COURT OF LAW

Bringing a Pedophile to Justice

A novel by

Lance K. Steele

Copyright © 2010

ALL RIGHTS RESERVED

ISBN   # 0982703120

EAN # 9780982703120

To those who have
lost someone
to a vicious,
conscienceless predator...
this book
is sincerely dedicated

DISCLAIMERS

✓ NAMES ARE FICTITIOUS; any similarities to real persons, places or things are coincidental.

✓ BEHAVIOR IS FICTITIOUS; real-life cops never lie, beat suspects in custody or bend the law. I made it all up. Likewise, prosecutors seek justice, not just convictions. And there's no such thing as a pedophile, either. Trust me; your kids are safe, probably studying algebra at a friend's place right now.

✓ ACTS OF DEPRAVITY FICTITIOUS; I made that shit up, too... no matter how gross, it never happened, *GOT IT?*

✓ IM A LYING SONOFABITCH; I made it all up. Everything I wrote is fabrication, prevarication, bullshit make-believe-pretend-stuff.

Seriously

INTRODUCTION

Years ago, I read about a great author of thrillers. I'd mention his name, but I don't want to get sued. Besides, I can't remember it. They asked him how he came up with such scary, gory shit for his stories. His answer inspired me. It went like this:

Steven told the interviewer; *"I just turn my mind loose. I take off the censors. I let my mind think up the ugliest, nastiest scenarios that I would never ever want to see happen… then I write it down."*

Well it worked for him. I hope it works for me. I raised a daughter and son; they're grown up, thank God, but back when they were tiny children, I had the typical fears most parents have; that someone would steal 'em and do horrible things to them.

So, for my first venture into scary books, I give you "Court of Law…" If it's not scary or graphic enough, perhaps I failed to get my mind dark enough to suit your twisted taste.

I'll try harder next time.

PREDATOR

David Eastbrook tried to remain calm as he sat there judging the high-kicking beauties. Being so close thrilled him, but there was also a second thrill. He sat between two other judges who hadn't the slightest suspicion. This forcing of discipline over lust heightened his kill-thrill; visual foreplay, governed by an extreme intellect and willpower.

He was at the peak of his game, his craft so polished that the cops would never catch him. It was almost too easy to feed his habit. Perhaps that is what brought him to the world of pageants; it reintroduced some of the risk of capture, like some folks screw in a public elevator to enhance their pathetic sex lives.

The pageant world exemplified everything wrong with an affluent society; people with superficial needs and the means with which to fulfill them. Parents pimping their kids to fulfill their voyeuristic fantasy, with little regard for the kid's well being... Shallow people imprinting hollow values, oblivious to the consequence.

The pageant world is the dog show gone mad; coifed hair, personal trainers, choreographers; seven-year-olds doing the bump 'n grind, finger-licks and pelvic thrusts while wearing a Shirley Temple smile. If it meant redefining the laws of child pornography, it was a small price to pay to win a tiara or get a TV shot.

And, to the delight of sexual predators, they paraded their daughters with style, smile and dimple before a sea of total strangers. It made Eastbrook smirk; a never-ending river of Barbies flowing before him on his personal catwalk. His life couldn't be more perfect, so long as he didn't blow his cover.

But he wouldn't. Each piece of camouflage was a heat shield tile on Shuttle-craft Eastbrook to insulate him from fiery re-entries. He spent most of his time held down by earthly constraints. His periodic hunts for satiation were the pre-launch and launch, demanding great care and planning.

Ah, then there was the orbiting; where he could float, alone in his cocoon with his frightened, naked mark. He loved the orbiting phase, when he was a god… omnipotent and without limits.

He wished the orbiting would never end, but sooner or later, the girl always died and his orbit would start to decay. Gravity sees to that. Spacecraft Eastbrook would dead-stick to a smoking halt on Terra Firma.

It only took one loose tile to kill a NASA shuttle and crew. Likewise, it would only take one loosened piece of Eastbrook's façade to bring him down in a fireball of retribution. He worked to keep it flawless.

Back when he mailed away for his ministerial degree from a Caribbean diploma mill, nobody suspected ministers… Priests, maybe, but ministers, never. Memorizing enough scripture to pass, he oiled his way into a small Bible Belt church as assistant preacher. He gave individual counseling sessions to prepubescent babes, innocently sitting on his lap, confiding. They were too young to know what was going on under that robe; that's why he had them on his lap.

Eastbrook organized retreats. Always taking a matronly female or two along to defray suspicion, these were little more than feeding frenzies; girls innocently casting pheromones to the wind; and the sinister minister was always downwind.

But God has a way of balancing the scales. And it came to pass that one day his robe fell from the hook, landing upside down for all to see. Dried semen told the tale, in the crudest of Biblical forensic terms.

The little church let him slip away; the last thing they needed was humiliation. Eastbrook milked the deal. They were eager to get rid of him; gave him a glowing recommendation so he could ply his trade *far away.*

He had little interest in women. They found it refreshing to meet a man that wasn't constantly on the make. This often put their daughters in his lap. Of course, a few were suspicious of any man that didn't want sex. A few presumed he was gay. He reinforced the presumption. A loose-wristed move here, an inflection there; opinions were automatically formed.

Wherever Eastbrook set up shop, he would establish early on that he was a toucher, working closely with girls. Having a baby girl on his lap was rarely suspected, and usually *expected.* In the rare events where suspicion surfaced, the trusting mothers actually defended their pastor. There was no way THEIR pastor would ever do anything like THAT. Denial is the taproot of the pedophile.

To men, he was invisible, like a mid-level executive, an embarrassment to hard men everywhere. He never played poker, ogled wives, hunted or fished. A man like that was invisible to Team Testosterone; first he'd have to fuck somebody's wife, poach a deer or start a fistfight.

He had a software company with offices across the South, creating goodwill and an excuse to be on the move; roving predators are harder to spot. He donated to PAL, charities, firefighters. If there was a pancake breakfast, he was flipping pancakes. If there were a dunking booth, Pastor Dave would be sitting on the trap. His altruistic camouflage only worked if everyone saw it enough to get bored with it.

And now at 57, he was at the peak of his game. He sold out to some dot com assholes for six times what it was worth. Naturally, he signed a five-year support deal; meaning five more years trolling the Deep South for little girls, those pretty little…

Just then, twenty-four legs went into a panties-flashing routine, snapping him back from his autobiographical reverie. He eyed the young beauties as a hungry dog eyes a t-bone steak sizzling on a grill… out of reach, but… oh, so tantalizing.

SEMIFINALS

He tried not to stare; that was the hard part. He could abduct, terrorize, rape and kill with the best of them. He could cover up the deed perfectly, but feigning disinterest *this close* to tender young girls? He had to suck the drool back, to keep his secret. Forcing his eyes to his clipboard, the information leaped at him. Girl Eleven, from Yuma; the choice for his next orbit.

Eagle Peaks would host their pageant three days later. Then it would be Saint Albion's the next week. Most parents would die before missing three consecutive pageants within easy driving range, so Miss Arizona would probably catch all three.

Soon, six semifinalists had been chosen. Two hundred forty four girls went home with broken hearted parents. Perhaps next time... after more lessons, choreography, personal training or whatever, but for the time being they were simply losers. No amount of titty glitter and sequins can hide it; *losing... really sucks.*

The six semifinalists reveled in glory. It wasn't every day that a girl made it to the semis in such a prestigious event. For lesser Barbies, making the Cottonwood semis would be grounds for bragging.

So, while most parents would take their kids out for pizza, for the lucky six, it would be lockdown, spinach salad and bottled water, then a briefing for the final round of combat.

That's what it was, too; a no-holds-barred, dog-eat-dog bout. Only one girl got the tiara. A stolen costume here, stepped-on violin bow there... it was just a question of getting away with it.

Last year's leader had it locked, until she danced her final ballet solo. The projectile diarrhea hit right in the middle of a toe spin, runny shit flailed off her tutu, splattering judges and front row spectators alike. But before she quit shitting, her parents cried foul. Blood work later proved someone slipped the kid a strong laxative. It was combat, all right... no shit.

And so the savvy finalist parents safeguarded their kids' food, instruments, clothing and makeup. One couple actually changed motels; motel staff had been known to take a bribe.

Morning finally came. The finalists paced, walking off butterflies, rehearsing lines for the most commonly asked impromptu questions, should they hear one.

But Eastbrook volunteered to write them, this time. Nobody wanted a trite question that might produce a monosyllabic answer. They had to be simple, yet sophisticated enough to prompt a credible soliloquy. The queries also had to be ORIGINAL, so no prior contestant had an advantage. If things went according to plan, he would be raping Little Miss Yuma in a few days. All he needed was an ambush site, hence the question.

It took just a little setup to get them to cheat. Hell, they were primed from two years of runner-ups. When they parked, Eastbrook got out of his car. Smiling his baby conning smile, he headed for the contestant's entrance; freshly written questions dangling from his clipboard. He was the Pied Piper; they were the rats.

Partially covering the list was a small Bible, whose bookmark was a synopsis of judging criteria; it looked like he had been on a higher spiritual plane, praying for divine guidance.

Brittanie scurried; her parents hurried to catch up to the judge. They'd seen him studying their daughter in prelims. They entered the elevator just right. Buffy's tits pressed firmly into the judge's fleshy dorsum. He inwardly sneered at the obvious bait, but pretended to be interested, leaning back. He thought briefly about expanding his killing; people like these needed it.

A smile flitted across his lips as his left hand, away from the husband, floated back and lifted her short skirt. Instantly finding her clit dead center, he began strumming lightly.

A surprised gasp almost got out of Buffy's mouth before she clipped it off; with her lame husband standing there, totally clueless, she reflexively pressed into the hand. The impromptu orgasm was her first in two years. She hated to admit it, but she wanted the soft judge. She hated the fingers when they withdrew. The elevator doors opened.

Brittanie was young, but had been mimicking the game in countless pageants. The look on her mother's face was one she'd never seen. It looked like anger but not quite; Mom covered it up fairly fast.

Lance was unaware. He was too busy peeking sideways at the queries. Perhaps if he had known, he might have approved; anything to gain favor with a senior judge.

Eastbrook added more bait; "Ah, we're early... Coffee and donuts over there. I shall be... *over there.*"

He indicated a door, barely out of sight from the pageant command post. It was a blatant invitation, as close as he could get to; *"I'm ready for a bribe, but keep it quiet"*.

It was what they needed to hear. They sent Brittanie backstage to warm up. They lingered until any roving eyes looked elsewhere. But it was overkill; no parent cared about the others. Buffy whisked through the door while Lance kept walking nonchalantly down the hall.

Eastbrook panicked when the woman entered alone. She stood there, conflicted by lust and shame for wanting to do it again. Then Lance entered. 'Spy v. Spy' had nothing on pageant parents.

Lance was tired of driving thousands of miles, coughing it up for costumes, trainers, lessons... and all to be nothing more than a runner-up dad. He decided to be blatant.

"Sir... what would it *take* to get a look *at those?*"

He wanted to ask if he could have their daughter; he was at a loss for a better answer. Doubt was in his eyes. Fortunately, the parents assumed he was reluctant about cheating.

Buffy softened it; "We saw you watching Brittanie; we know you like her for a podium. We'll do *ANYTHING*. We can keep quiet, too."

He knew the parents had but one goal; making their Barbie famous. They could live off her table scraps. Hell, that was the plan for every pageant parent; make the kid a star at all costs... then surf the fame-wave.

He downplayed it; "Well, uh, it's not like we're doing anything *WRONG,* really; everybody's going to see them soon... Your daughter just sees them a little earlier. *Is that so wrong?"*

Both parties relaxed; a deal seemed imminent.

Compared to spiking a kid's food, this was kid's stuff.

"It's a lonely life on tour, even for judges. Buy me a nice dinner, a few days down the road... and *nobody knows about it?*"

Their heads nodded in unison. Fuck Yes! Dinner it would be! They hastily copied, Lance taking the odd, Buffy the even questions. Then Lance cracked the door, checking if it was clear to leave.

"Lance, I need to speak to the judge... privately."
"OK, Honey Bun, see you backstage."
Lance D. Rutherford didn't have a clue.
The 'D' stood for Denial.

She blasted Eastbrook.
"What happened... in the elevator *NEVER HAPPENED, understand?*"

He saw conflict, indignation and passion swirling; a dangerous combination, which always brought unpredictable action. Far better for one emotion to dominate. He had fucked women before, but took no joy in it; They had demands. They were hairy down there. But in the elevator, he learned she shaved... she almost felt like a young girl.

He hurried to conjure an image of Buffy's naked daughter, bleeding and pleading. It got him hard immediately. He grabbed the tight-skirted yuppie bitch, pressing her buttocks against the desk. Moaning, she thrust her pelvis at the pervert. For a soft man, he was surprisingly hard. Buffy came twice in rapid succession. The whole thing was hot and fast...just the way she'd wanted it. She left as though nothing ever happened; just one more sacrifice for Brittanie. As she approached Lance, he finished reading the impromptu questions.

"Hey, Buff… what do you make of this one?"
Buffy glanced around first.
"6. When you're on the road, where do you like to stay, and what do you like to do?"

Brittanie practiced clarinet while the parents worked on her spontaneous answer. Nobody wanted to know that they stayed in Economizers, that the bulimic little brat disgorged pizza or that she held cops in contempt. Finally they had her impromptu answer down pat.

"I like to stay with my parents in Mariposa Hotels and when I get the chance, I help sick children in hospitals… but the circuit keeps me pretty busy."
She finished with curtsy and cutesy dimples.

Four hours later, Brittanie made the final three. As fate would have it, she was last to be interviewed. Meanwhile, Lance and Buffy churned with turmoil. The first two contestants obviously previewed the secret queries also. Worse yet, they disgorged the same bullshit; world peace, volunteering to help old folks, sick kids or homeless… Brittanie would go down in flames, a third-rate copycat. The parents could only watch helplessly as their future starlet would crash and burn… *again.*

But Brittanie figured it out. If she *HAD to lose*, she vowed do it with style. Shit-canning the prepared answer, she decided to go with honesty; desperate times call for desperate measures.

There were only three judges for the finals; Eastbrook, Ursula Upton, a stodgy old Orick schoolmarm and the grand high-exalted ruler, the ex-Reverend, Augustus J. Hightower. The panel was privy to contestants' questionnaires, portfolios and damned near everything else needed to get the goods on a family; a pedophile's perfect perch.

When Judge Upton asked, Brittanie threw caution to the wind.

"When I'm on the road... where do I *LIKE TO STAY, and WHAT DO I LIKE TO DO?* Well, we stay at those Economy hotels, because they're cheap; it costs a lot to be on tour. We get a discount for early reservations; in fact, we already have ours for the next two pageants! Now, what do I like to do? I talk on my cell to my girlfriends. When I'm not training, I love pizza! *That's all!"*
She posed curtsy, dimples and tee-hee giggle.

The panel struggled with her honesty, since nobody had ever tried it before. But of the three judges, Eastbrook alone took special note; Econolodge, next weekend, already reserved. Little Miss Yuma finished first runner-up, a career high.

Ten days later while the other pageant Barbies posed in St. Albion's prelims, authorities identified the remains of Brittanie Rutherford. Judge Dave Eastbrook never did get that free dinner.

But then, he'd had something better.

Five weeks later...

BUG

The first blowfly smelled the proteinacious death messengers just minutes after the body was dumped. She preferred the eyes or mouth, but those sites were still frozen. The vagina would do. Ovipositor quivering and contracting rhythmically, soon three hundred tiny white eggs adorned the largest labial laceration.

She found a safe perch; many other blowflies were just as eager to lay their eggs and get back to hiding. It was a bug-eat-bug world, no place for a blowfly to be exposed. By sunset, the body hosted five thousand eggs, each wound a frosty-rimmed margarita of death. The insects went dormant, awaiting sunshine.

But there was more at work than insects, in the decomposition of Tiffany Michelle Simpson's body. The "First Stage of Decomposition" is life; millions of bacteria in the GI tract break down starches, proteins and lipids. Without these user-friendly bacteria, a human would starve to death with a gut full of food.

But upon death, they turn their digestive enzymes on the intestinal wall. They eat the GI tract first, then the other organs. So while the insect world awaited the sun, the bacteriofauna ate and reproduced; darkness be damned.

RAT

Just before the moon rose, a wood rat appeared. Earlier, she'd heard the heavy footsteps of a human from the safety of her nest. Three feet high, six in diameter, it was a crude arrangement of larger branches on bottom, then gnawed-off blackberry vines. On top of that, twigs of poison oak, Chemise, pin oak or coyote brush; anything that was nearby and dry.

Inside were two chambers; one a decoy, lined with prickly Live Oak leaves. Its stealthiest archenemy, the diamondback, would make noise crawling over that stuff, giving her time to exit the panic tunnel.

The main chamber was where the rat ate, slept and nursed litters. It was lined with anything to ward off the cold and wet. Shredded cardboard was nice. So were feathers, hair and shredded bark. After rearing a brood, the room always needed clean lining to minimize risk of predation.

The earlier man sounds and power steering screech offered hope; humans meant food scraps and cardboard. The moon would rise soon, making her more vulnerable to predators. With ears swiveling for coyotes, eyes alternately scouring the dark sky for owls, she scurried from shadow to shadow, then chewed off a fair hunk of blanket. She hated the man stench in the microfibers, but it beat shredding bark.

COYOTE

The coyote smelled clues while trotting; puke-rich exhaust clung to sage, rubber tires mashed into the dry soil, even the stinking odors of the pervert. Six years of dodging leghold traps, varmint callers, pipe traps, county trappers, hungry pumas and trigger-happy plinkers with .22's honed his survival instincts to razor edge; it was a harsh place for songdogs.

Canis Latrans has a great sense of smell, over 90 times as good as man's. The Coastal Mountain summit reeked; lizards, pigmy rabbits, cottontails, jacks, quail, shitbirds and various reptiles. Of particular interest were mice, rabbits and fruit. But this was early fall, so prunes and peaches were still unreachable. That left him with staples, mice and rabbits. This particular loop, twelve miles long, rarely held much, but the next drainage over was one of his favorite hunting grounds.

The coyote slunk into a belly-crawl as the basin came into view. Five minutes of careful circling brought him downwind and below. He smelled the sexual predator's stench; sweat, shit, wine and cheese, but it was stale. The man was gone.

The downdraft also carried a female's scent; dead, almost breeding age, ate a ham sandwich and milk, hours before dying. Whiffs of urine and adrenaline; the female was afraid before she died.

The coyote lifted his nose one more time; he sniffed no pipe traps or trapper's cover-up. It had been four years since a leg-hold took his mate, but the vanilla cover-up burned into his scent memory.

Still suspicious, he had to trust his nose if he was to eat. He trotted within five yards of the half-buried

corpse. He wasn't hungry enough yet to eat dead humans. Catching a wood rat whiff, he was tempted to follow, but digging rats always left his paws full of thorns. He trotted toward his happy hunting grounds. Maybe he'd get lucky over in the thick brush; he liked cottontails.

RAVEN

The horizon slowly illuminated, awakening the raven. It, too, was curious about the strange noises the evening before. His coarse wingtips beat a raspy cadence in the high country air.

The sharp eyes spotted two shiny discs. He split-essed and folded its wingtips, doing snap rolls. There was no sense losing altitude without having a little fun in the process; the raven is the skateboarder of the skies.

Flaring three feet from the soil, the pilot put his wings into anhedral sweep for a perfect harrier landing, just six inches from the shiny targets. He waddled closer; his sharp beak breached the closest eye, then the other. Cold vitreous humor slowly oozed down both cheeks. The eyes lost their shape and became drab, imploding gelatinous puddles. The raven quickly lost interest; apparently, the shiny metallic discs were nothing worth eating or stealing.

He flew off in search of other things to play with. The day was full of promise for the curious, fun-loving supercrow.

BUZZARDS

They spent the night on their favorite perch, a dead White Oak high on the ridge where it caught the earliest sunlight. In California, where summer temperatures fluctuate fifty degrees between day and night, such a perch can mean the difference between life and death; the early bird gets the maggot.

So the mated pair patiently held their fog-soaked wings at half-mast, pointing their backs at the sun, steam vapors rising like campfire smoke. In a few more minutes they'd be dry enough to reacquire their normal wing loading of six ounces per square foot, again capable of a glide ratio of sixty-to-one.

The high vantage gave another benefit; they might see peers soaring. When colleagues soar, that is one thing, but when they soar, it means food. They could lock wings, glide over and join in a bonanza.

Rarely, they sniffed an easy meal while perched. This was one of those mornings. The dead thing was fresh and close. They scanned horizons for competition. Finally, both birds were ready for flight. They did suicides and locked wings six feet under the perch. It was effortless and damned nearly silent.

They soared, merely yards above the rocks, like airborne bloodhounds. Several passes brought them to the steady scent. They tightened their search, staying under the summits to keep the secret to themselves. When they hit the big meadow, stench lingered throughout, making it impossible to pinpoint the source; the buzzards' equivalent to being in a forest fire. Too much smoke to spot the flames.

They perched. Buzzards can always wait. It took only half an hour before the shifting winds formed into a predictable updraft. Their meal happened to be a human body this time. The male folded pinions, dropped to six feet before spreading his outer panels, soaring closely over her. His nose said there wasn't any danger, but she wasn't ripe yet.

He made a few wingbeats and rejoined his mate on a suitable uphill perch. It wouldn't cost them another wingbeat to monitor the food; no other buzzards would see them soaring and circling. It wasn't even noon yet, and the pair had found a windfall. The day looked good for two veteran carrion eaters.

DAY TWO

New flies had to settle for lesser sites. Some crawled inside the external nares, wading through eggs to get to fresh turf. The meekest had to settle for exterior blood pools and thawing slime strands; definitely a crapshoot, but any brood is better than no brood.

The body looked fairly normal, save for a slightly swollen abdomen, pecked-out eyes, vitreous humor trickles and the thin white frosting of eggs on every orifice and wound. Its calm demeanor belied the underlying foment; half a billion germs, soon to be ten billion, and a hundred thousand writhing fly larvae.

Next came meat bees, powerful mandibles swiftly cutting tongue, eyelids and lips, then flying the protein back to the ground hive, stimulating the queen to lay eggs faster. Meatpackers Local #309 was in full swing.

The first maggot wave hatched; measuring one-tenth of an inch, First Instars have two ends... The front, having just hooks and spiracles, is made for eating. Its rear is for breathing and shitting. In between lies the bulk, whose only purpose is to turn protein into a fly.

By nightfall they molt again. The maggot is now a Second Instar, 2-5mm in length. It feeds voraciously upon anything. In regards to the dead body of Tiffany M. Simpson, gusto was the watchword.

DAY THREE

The second maggot wave hatched. Meat bees formed an aerial river, ferrying sequential bits of digitized Tiffany back to the hungry hive. Magpies and bluejays began chipping away morsels, chatting eagerly about the windfall. The belly heaves and swells with germs, their gaseous byproducts and rapid metabolism extrudes the tongue and colon.

The buzzards sniffed the robust yet refreshingly piquant linger of methane, hydrogen sulfide and just today, the odors that drive buzzards to new heights of ecstasy, putrescene and cadaverine… their equivalent to Parmesan on hot pizza; irresistible.

The female poked a testing peck on the right upper quadrant. Gas drove tiny liver-parts skyward. Almost as quickly as it erupted, the liver geyser reduced to a mere oozing trickle. The vultures wasted no time in elongating the wound so both featherless necks could fit… a vulture laparoscopy.

They wanted tissue that was just about ready for maggots, yet still had enough structure to be called tissue. Eagerly tearing and swallowing chunks of liver and rotting bowel, they were oblivious to all else.

Tiffany's body had been sending out odor too long. A young male circled, kicked out of the nest just two months ago. He was unsure if he should approach the adult pair alone; others saw him circling. Soon eleven buzzards grew in collective courage. They landed en mass; last one down's a rotten egg… eater.

Squawking and posturing proved pointless. The others were too hungry to be bluffed from such a fine meal. Feathers and dust flew over the windfall. The old pair lost; the corpse was common domain.

Some tasks are better completed with numbers. The partially interred food was inaccessible to more than three hungry beaks, so they pulled together. The body slid sixty yards down slope, slamming against bushes and rocks, spilling maggots, ooze and germs. The y eagerly attacked all fresh points of entry. Thanks to wildly splayed legs, each orifice got a hungry beak. The throat likewise got a famished featherless head.

By sundown, buzzards gulped thirty percent of the corpse weight. The bulk of their feast was over; they avoid shank, wrists and calves. It is simply too much work for too little reward. So when times are good and gutpiles plentiful, they soar off for easier meals.

MORNING 4

Continued scavenging exposed new sites, but when these last eggs hatched, they would starve on dry bones and sun-scorched soil. Still, nature courts chaos. The maggot mass heaved and writhed; undulating, reeking putrefaction... its heat from friction and metabolism aiding tissue breakdown, lengthening feeding hours, to consume ten percent of the body weight per day.

The first wave, now an inch long, crawled off the body to find hiding places, to harden and reach full pupae in four days. It would be ten days before adults emerged to repeat the cycle.

That is, assuming the pupa survives. This day brought parasitoids and flesh flies. They weren't picky about shank meat, brains or hard to reach extremity flesh. Homing in on maggot scent, the wasps lay eggs in maggots, pre-pupae and pupae. They would pupate and emerge as adults.

The first wave of Rove Beetles hit the corpse just before nightfall, Staphylinids having migrated robotically toward the putrefaction smells for some time. The turd-shaped beetles with their huge heads looked like black maggots wearing red helmets.

Before dark, feeding was at fever pitch; maggots sucking juice, beetles eating maggots, wasps and bees carrying off corpse meat, eggs and first instars. Still others fed on fatty tissues and exposed tendons. The only thing that slowed the carnage was darkness; after that, only beetles and intestinal germs kept working.

DAYS 5-15

The next ten days saw more Fourth Instars leave to pupate, parasitoids and Staphylinids feeding and laying eggs, birds, spiders and wasps raiding maggots with zeal. The body of Tiffany M. Simpson kept shriveling to comparative nothingness.

There were fewer bugs but more variety; new predatory wasps and beetles ravaging Fourth Instars, laying their eggs to complete their cycle again.

Tiny mites went for the skin and hair, competing with Hide Beetles. By the beginning of the third week in the searing autumn sun, the body was ready to accept carcass beetles of the family Troglidae; specialized feeders of tendons, ligaments and articular surfaces.

BOAR

The breeding class boar normally avoided carrion, but at a summer weight of only 235, he was lean, mean and real fuckin' hungry; he'd need another hundred pounds to survive winter.

There was a boom in turkey and squirrel populations, and those bastards got most of the acorns. The hog hated squirrels; the twitchy bastards could climb and take what they wanted, while the boar had to wait for the tasty nuts to drop. And those sharp-eyed birds ate his acorns, too. He killed turkeys whenever he got the chance, just for a little payback. The only thing better was eating their acorn-stuffed gizzards and shittin' on their torsos.

In hard times the pig resorted to fallback foods, rooting concrete-hard ground, turning logs to snort grubs, lizards and any vermin foolish enough to try to hide from his keen sniffer.

Still, there were many pigs but only so many unturned logs. He spent last week cannibalizing piglets in the next draw. That held other benefits; he got to fuck sows and kick ass on subordinate boars.

But a breeding class boar needs more than alligator lizards and a few hapless shoats to fuel his travels. He snorted the pupae. He tried to eat the right wrist, but the butyric acid scent turned him off; he wasn't *that hungry*, just yet.

The girl's exposed left femur pointed up, at a convenient height. Tentatively mouthing the distal femur, he positioned the epiphysis firmly against his favorite bone-busting middle molars. He began to bear down when it made a gratifying crack. He was glad for the change of flavors; marrow beats rattlers; they usually bit him, and then his face would be sore for a week. He ate the right epiphysis, but it didn't taste as good. Soon tiring of the flavor, he trotted off for the next drainage. There was a good spring over there, and usually sows to fuck.

FINDING THE CORPSE

Earl Pembrose had been bowhunting wild pigs for twenty years, without dogs. To Earl, it seemed chickenshit to use dogs. The boar can kick doggie ass all day long, so he seeks suitable terrain for a sporting joust. He butts up against a bluff and readies his business end; a few quick tusk slashes ought to do it.

But the boar is thinking about a fair fight; one or two dogs... Soon a dog grabs an ear. Another dog grabs the other. Worse yet, a hound clamps on his nuts. Then men arrive; they kill the courageous warrior. Then they stitch up the hounds and go home, proud of their courage. Definitely a chickenshit way to kill such a worthy adversary. If they hunted African Lions like that, it would be outlawed.

Compared to that, Earl would arrive before daylight, sit on the tailgate sipping coffee, listening for anything that might herald a mature boar. They like to fight and breed in cool predawn summer mornings. Squealing and roaring accompany both activities; sometimes Earl would hear them, then stalk within range.

Usually he heard nothing, so he'd stillhunt to locate pigs. Seeing pigs is enough for the rifleman; the trigger is pressed and the hog dies, but for the bowhunter, seeing a pig is just the beginning. Special attention to wind is vital; not just the breeze, but eddies, thermals, downdrafts; one whiff of man scent will put any boar to flight or fight.

Ten minutes earlier, he thought he'd heard a cracking sound, like when pigs crack black walnuts; the sound was hard to locate it or even be sure if he heard it at all. So he stalked the noise and hoped. Optimism is a bowhunter's best tool.

Five hundred yards and two ridges later, he smelled the beast or its travel line. Knowing that breeder-class boars travel like locomotives, he extrapolated the course and ran as quietly as possible to head it off.

A single Manzanita branch wiggled. The increasing light finally showed it. The boar stood behind the small bush, tail twitching excitedly at the subterranean meal. The wind was right, luckily.

The brush obliterated vitals. Lacking a clean killing shot, Earl held still, hoping the pig would offer the only killing shot; a double lung broadside. He nocked an arrow and drew the bow silently.

"Pick a spot… PICK a spot…"

Knowing how easy it is to miss a gravy shot by shooting at the whole animal, Earl would pick the second rib back from the shoulder blade; when the arrow-stopping scapula moved forward, he would dump the string and he would follow through smoothly.

Soon the boar stepped from behind the Manzanita, chomping on Indian Soap, which explains why he didn't hear the string noise. The shaft blew through his lungs. Hearing the graphite slam against the bushes on the far side, he thought another boar was charging; he whirled to face his imaginary enemy, raising guard hairs, swaying left and right, grunting a challenge. Just as he started popping tusks, his lungs collapsed and he went to sleep, dead before his resin-stained tusks hit the ground.

Earl watched the whole thing without nocking another arrow; it was too intense and over too fast. He had taken his biggest boar; he could hardly wait to go and claim it. There was just one problem... His legs were jelly. He sat back and reached in his pack for coffee. Savoring the brew, he enjoyed the pastel sunrise. There would be time for field dressing soon enough.

But before he finished his coffee it dawned on him; in his haste to give chase, he forgot his pig tags in the truck, along with his field dressing kit. He backtracked the boar's trail and headed for the truck. Fairly near his truck he stumbled on the remains of Tiffany Simpson. The field dressing would have to wait.

DUMPSITE

Deputy Sheriffs Ann Baxter and Ed Landon were the nearest law, so they responded; Dispatch said a hunter happened upon human remains. It took a few wrong turns on unmarked dirt roads, but they got there in fairly good time.

The impatient hunter didn't look like a suspect; his driver license, registration, proof of insurance, hunting license and pig tags were good. He led them to the body. It was steep as hell and treacherous. They instructed Pembrose to leave and keep quiet about it.

Ed knew things about bones, since he had earlier wanted to become a chiropractor, so he studied comparative anatomy and zoology before the law bug bit him. After that, all thoughts of drugless healthcare left him. Chicks dig guns and badges.

It had to be a young girl, judging from the wide pubic angle and light bone structure. Surmising that it slid downhill, they studied the slope. Ed spotted the cheap plated necklace, one word stamped into it; *"Shelly."*

Slipping and grabbing brush to keep from falling, they hiked up to the vestiges of a skid road. They spotted the grave; they were looking at a homicide.

"Ann, get the camera and bags from the truck."
"Yeah."
They never commanded each other, but the imperative was lost on both of them. She called it in and grabbed the gear.

Before she exited, the radio squawked back.

"Five six nine, stand by…"

Baxter was impressed at the quick comeback.

"Ten four, 69 standing by."

Baxter liked the resonating baritone of James Three Feathers, the finest coroner they ever had; there was no ambiguity or distraction when he broadcast.

"Five Six Nine, what have you got, over?"

"Probable homicide, up near Red Mountain. Looks like it's been here a couple-three weeks, maybe more; what you want us to do? Over."

Three Feathers processed quickly; probably a drug deal gone bad or the vic stumbled on a pot patch or meth lab. Considering it was almost harvest time, he put his money on the Pot angle.

In his youth, Three Feathers had hunted every damned ankle-busting mile of that ridge. Just thinking of the steep slippery terrain made his bad knee hurt.

"Five Six Nine, shoot it, tag it, bag it… over."

"Ten Four. We're out."

She felt good… Her boss trusted them to bring in the body. Either that or Jimmy just didn't want to slip and slide all over the damned hillside. They documented, bagged thre remains and every trace they could see. Then they sifted, coming up with a few errant phalanges and the Hyoid bone, which was obviously fractured.

AUTOPSY

James Three Feathers wasn't like the coroners on TV. He wouldn't eat over a corpse or make jokes. He had respect for the Great Spirit that resided in all things. He rarely allowed visitors, but he liked this young white woman; she had something special. He narrated the particulars; date, his name and tag number.

"Partial skeleton, Caucasian female, approximately ten to twelve, judging by the Iliac Crest Sign and femoral capital epiphyseal growth sign." That much was obvious; white skin tags, wide pelvis and growth plates that weren't ossified. So far, a no-brainer.

"Body has been extensively scavenged. Both lower legs are missing. Distal femoral endplates are absent, with diaphyseal splintering approximately one-fifth the way up the right femur and slightly further on the left. The ends are bloodless, suggesting splintering was post mortem and indicative of scavenging by either a bear, wild boar or possibly puma."

The big sheriff's eyes moved up the torso.

"Internal organs are not available, due to decomp, weathering and scavenging. The thoracic cavity is dry to touch, essentially unremarkable. Moving up the spine, I find the normal 12 Dorsal vertebrae, twelve pairs of ribs and seven cervical vertebrae."

Then he spotted it.

"Correction; fifth and sixth cervical vertebrae are non-segmented, suggesting congenital-developmental anomaly."

He shut off the tape and spoke quietly to Baxter.

"Non-segmentation is fairly common, affecting 2-4% of the population. It's of only minor clinical importance to chiropractors who motion-palpate for paired coupling. But it holds more relevance in death; might help identify this body."

Knowing that spinal anomalies usually occur in clusters, he went to the lower lumbar spine as he turned the mike back on.

"A corresponding anomaly is noted at the posterior aspect of the L-5 vertebra; a spina bifida occulta."

He turned off the tape; didn't want to record his initial opinion, lest he get nailed to that cross later in court.

"This victim probably had a birth mark over it; it's associated with SBO, dark in pigmentation on Whi... *Caucasians* and it's really hairy. Her parents would be aware; might be on her birth records, too."

Ann Baxter liked him more, seeing the depth of experience; the skull saw buzzed.

"Judging from the odor, maggots and beetles scavenged the intracranial tissues. The confines of the calvarium are smooth and regular; no evidence of fracture or trauma is seen."

Jimmy dumped the bags on the table. "Scene examination by Officers Landon and Baxter produced several bones; three proximal phalanges and the Pisiform are noted, all from the right hand. They are normal. I note that the Hyoid bone is fractured."

He used his magnifying glass.

"I note dried blood in the fracture ends."
Again, he turned the recorder off.

"You see this blood, on the ends? This is highly vascularized; the kid was growing fast. You wouldn't see it on an adult's, but... anyhow, her heart was pumping when this bone broke. The only way is from strangulation."

He turned the tape back on.
"This fracture is suggestive of strangulation, and pending new data to the contrary, it is my opinion that this victim died from strangulation."
He shut off the tape and made notes while speaking.

"Ann, you're looking for a lost daughter, taken about four weeks, maybe longer. Judging from this necklace, her name was Shelly or Michelle. She was blond, about five one to five-four, 85-100 with a dark, hairy birthmark in the midline of her low back. Aside from that, she was strangled, and probably raped. I'm sorry."

"So am I."

The conversation was over. Baxter left for her office. The coroner went to his desk to finish his paperwork.

IDENTIFICATION

She went online, finding Shelly quickly; blond, blue, missing for almost four weeks, pink blouse, white skirt, nameplate necklace and earrings. The only thing missing were earrings... souvenirs, maybe.

Mendonesia County notified Gander City PD that a body matching Tiffany Michelle Simpson awaited DNA, dental records and whatever else to confirm or rule out. Soon the fax disgorged fingerprints, medical records. Sure enough, hairy birthmark, mid-line, low back.

Photographs printed out next. Baxter didn't have the heart to tell them her db was just a skeleton, not in need of photographic ID. She walked the records over to Jimmy; pending DNA, it was likely Simpson's body.

Baxter looked at the photos; feather boa, makeup, titty glitter, fake nails, pro hairdo. The only things this Barbie didn't have were the fake cones. If she had lived to the ripe old age of fourteen, she assumed the implants would've been in place, too.

Such photos sent the wrong message to the kids, reinforcing superficial qualities that women rights activists had been trying to abolish since the seventies. It objectified her. It made her bait. To the unbalanced psyche, it would seem she was put there specifically for his own sick amusement.

Finishing her shift, Baxter called her partner for support.
"Hey, Landon, how 'bout I buy you a drink... or two?"
"You got it, partner! I'll see you in fifteen."

ABDUCTION

For the first time in months, he felt fulfilled. He relived raping that little bitch from Yuma. He replayed it over and over, masturbating to the thoughts. The whole event had been perfect. His camouflage was perfect; the parents wouldn't ever suspect him... Not that asshole husband; he was too fixated on the pageants.

His wife wouldn't make the connection either; first, there would be grieving. Then if she DID think back, she'd probably repress her contact with Eastbrook. And if there were any lingering sexual issues, she could get all the cock she wanted in good old Yuma.

With time, he got restless again. He tossed and turned. He woke up several times a night with the same face in his dreams; blond-haired, blue-eyed, cheap jewelry. Her lips pouted slightly, like a big, filthy pussy that needed something shoved into it.

The dreams increased in frequency and intensity. Soon he would have to rape again. That was the only time he felt normal; after a good raping. At first, he resisted. Later, he acknowledged it. Finally, he caved to it and rationalized his flaw; he wasn't bad, really, he was just sick. The only treatment was raping and killing his dream girl. Then after the treatment wore off, the dreams would return, keep getting worse until he self-medicated again.

To Eastbrook, this was acceptable. There was an unlimited supply of young girls out there. For the skilled organized pedophile, acquisition was surprisingly easy. So, if the experts were right and he really did have a disease, fortunately the cure was easy and fun. There was just one problem; the highs weren't so high and the post-kill normalcy periods were shortening.

He knew that addiction cycles were like that. It takes more drugs to get high, then just to feel normal, and finally, just to avoid feeling sick. Ultimately, the substance... *whatever it is,* kills the addict.

He tried to up the dosage by inflicting more pain on his victims, but it didn't work; they were already scared shitless. He tried to vary his methods, but his behavior was an indelible signature.

His only option was to increase frequency of treatment. This was not entirely unpleasant, much as a half-drunk person chooses to drink more to avoid a hangover, so Eastbrook stepped up the frequency.

Avalon's Agency worked with plenty of future starlets. They had been pestering him to give a seminar for elite clients; what judges look for, things to avoid, success tips, etc. He finally agreed.

Avalon's notified their elite clients. Three Saturdays hence, David I. Eastbrook, judge of future stars, benevolent socialite and generous philanthropist would bestow upon them all things pageant.

Avalon's thrilled at the thought. They had no idea that one of their clients would soon be dead because of their actions. Had they known, it is doubtful they would've cared; Eastbrook was a hellofa judge...

Jennifer Simpson opened the mailbox. Junk mail went into her left hand, bills into the right, while she walked to her split-level; the only spoils from the divorce. The lavender flier didn't fit either hand. She had been trying to get Tiffany into Avalon's Inner Circle. She tore open the flier; big-time judge, ten-percent off for pre-registration. She grabbed her phone and credit card; anything for an edge.

The days passed swiftly.

He took the introduction in stride. With all of those girls sitting so close, it was hard not to squirm. He stayed focused by charming the mothers, mesmerized by his seductive words of promise. By the end of the seminar, they'd let him drive their girls home. He was smooth.

They left with pearls of wisdom. He left with something, too. Her application said she was perfect; long legs, skinny frame, long blond hair, sky-blue eyes and china-white teeth. She was ten and a half; she went to J.F.K, six blocks from Eastbrook's home, so she might walk to and from. He'd stay home, to check it out.

On Tuesday morning his hopes materialized; Tiffany and a young boy walked past his house. She moved confidently, as though practicing for a gig on some future catwalk; yeah, a catwalk. They disappeared.

It occurred to him; she and her mother knocked on his door, selling candies for a fundraiser about a year ago. She was too young then, but now she was perfect. It wouldn't be long before she was writhing in pain. He began planning for launch; thrills filled his guts.

He never took girls near home, so this would be the exception; he needed a scapegoat. He booted his laptop and quickly found three pedophiles within half a mile of Simpson's place. He didn't give the first one a second thought.

Jeremy Thornhill had only one conviction, stat rape. Of course, the People didn't care about the first fifty or sixty times they fucked. They were both minors.
Then Jeremy turned eighteen, but his sweetheart was still just fifteen. True, it wasn't what the legislators had in mind when they created statutory rape law, but convictions to a DA are eggs to a hen; the more, the merrier; stepping-stones to higher office.

He took a plea; consequently, a host of opportunities were no longer available. Men with that label can never shake it. Meanwhile, he married his sweetheart and they tried to make the most of it.

On the other hand, Sandoval was convicted at twenty-eight; got five years, but thanks to an overcrowded penal system, was released early. Eight months later he was convicted for offenses on twins, but the judge overturned the verdict due to a chain of evidence breach. Even the judge must've hated that. Before he dismissed, he had to remind the angry gallery; it was a court of LAW, not revenge.

Two years later, Sandoval got popped again. He had a twelve-year-old boy in his van, when the rear doors swung open; an off-duty cop thwarted the rape.

Ironically, the cop paradoxically saved Sandoval from hard time; the state couldn't prove Sandoval had coerced the child; he hadn't been penetrated, gagged or bound. The only good thing? He saved the kid... assuming he wanted saving; some didn't.

Sandoval had many forced stints at counseling, chemical castration, behavior modification; predictably, results were pathetic. The hardened sexual predator has the poorest recidivism rate of all. The only cure is a bullet to the brain or lethal injection. However, nobody wants to admit correctional system failure. Better to let more children suffer than to exterminate the vermin that stalk them.

So Eastbrook went with the real estate catch phrase; location, location, location. Crystobal Sandoval, aka "Greasy Chris," would be the scapegoat, purely due to proximity and profile; no impulse control, long rap sheet. He was practically strapped to the death gurney.

He needed to stalk Sandoval, to find his windows of opportunity, where Sandoval had no alibi. He called his second in command.

"Bernie? Dave here."

"Oh, *HI, Dave*... what's up?"

"I need to swing over to the Vegas branch for a few days. You've got the bridge, number one."

"Aye, Captain... *bridge it is!*"

Bernard Davis swelled with pride; Boss remembered he loved Star Trek. Number One would run the Enterprise, all by himself, for *'a few days'*... He never had a boss as cool as Dave.

Sandoval was easy to stalk; he slept in until ten thirty. He walked past the schoolyard; one mile beyond was a strip mall. The near end had a quick stop, Mexican food store, Laundromat and at the far end, an adult bookstore.

True, porn shops weren't supposed to be near schools, but the shop was there first; it was grandfathered. Chalk up a black eye and maroon cock ring for unbridled urban sprawl.

Sandoval would buy coffee and donuts, saunter to the porn shop, find a private booth and whack off to kiddy porn. Later he'd buy a bottle and walk home. Around four, he'd be drinking, with Latino music blaring from his old wooden console TV-stereo, a holdover from the seventies. The snoring would start around six.

After seeing the same routine for three days straight, Eastbrook had him patterned; Greasy Chris had no friends, job or ambition other than donuts, alcohol and kid porn. The asshole was perfect for Eastbrook's plan.

COUNTDOWN

The RV was a tremendous tool for the killer; he blended wherever he went. The high-end RV's very opulence insulated him from suspicion.

The windows were too high for snoopers, making it a perfect torture chamber. Its security cameras on the roof could scan a fifty-yard perimeter. Inside, a pair of cameras covered the bed, so he could film his deeds.

He liked his chest freezer. He fed the contractor some bullshit about going to Alaska to catch salmon and halibut, to bring gourmet meat back home. But the installer didn't give a shit; he'd put weirder shit into RV's... weirder by a damn sight.

But the freezer would never see a fish scale. After killing a child he would freeze it. Maggots can't eat frozen food; entomological timelines get skewed. Liver temperature, putrefaction and desiccation rates would all be worthless. Should there ever come a trial, the altered forensics might aid his defense by distorting the actual time of death.

There was just one flaw. If the body were found before it thawed, even the rankest ME would smell a rat. Fortunately all of his priors thawed and were ravaged. He credited luck and planning for his perfect record.

Normally, he liked stealing marks before school; in Southern California, most couples work two jobs, it was unlikely either parent was home to take the school's call. By the time the parents got word, Eastbrook and his mark would be gone.

His second choice was after school. Assuming the parents were home and interested, would waste precious time calling her friends, asking about sleepovers, dates and parties before calling the cops. By then, it would be dark, Eastbrook's favorite time. Darkness covered a lot.

Until recently, police felt justified in delaying action on missing children reports; the kid was usually with buddies, at a party or one ex forgot to tell the other about taking the kid. So the wisest use of police resources was to not squander them too soon.

But after several famous abductions pointed out this administrative Bermuda Triangle, public pressure forced law enforcement to modify protocol; the first hours were golden for catching perverts. Now, if the cops smelled abduction, they could act quickly.

He recalled the mixture of fear and elation when the Amber Alerts posted a girl that he actually had in his freezer while he drove past; he reveled in the irony.

He figured he might have four hours on the short side, before they came to to ask; *"Have you seen this girl?"* On the long side, it might be a full day; especially if Sandoval played his role properly.

At last he decided to steal Simpson after school.

BLAST OFF

Tiffany sat in class watching a movie, bored as usual. She was going to be a star. Stars didn't need school; they needed big tits, firm ass and the guts to shake it onstage. Well, she didn't have the tits yet, but she would someday.

The movie was the same one she'd seen last year; *"It's OK to say NO to Uncle Joe."* The film was lauded for its success in alerting children.

But really, it didn't do dick. It had the same flaw that all such programs had. Straight-thinking people made the film, but they never venture into the dark corners of the psyche. Honest, moral people can't conceive the ways of the pervert, much less circumvent them. It takes a crook to catch a crook.

There was the condescending nature of such films. They talked to children as though they were already safe. This of course, is patently untrue, and it turns children off. Without an element of danger in a story, no child worth saving will listen. Fear catalyzes the learning process like no other enzyme.

Countless civilizations exploited fear to teach children critical survival lessons. From trolls to poison apples and cannibalistic witches, fear rings our bell the loudest. School administrations should honor this time-tested method for teaching life lessons, but instead they chose the opposite... and they fail.

It isn't politically correct to scare children shitless. So instead of exploiting fear, showing the real-world evil of sexual predators and their snares, they try to teach about evil without illustrating evil per se. Boredom is a poor instructor. Perhaps that's why Tiffany allowed herself to be abducted.

So she sat there, waiting for the bell. Her mind drifted to tomorrow; she had a session at Avalon's with a new choreographer, thanks to that seminar last week with that judge.

After what seemed like years, she was free at last! She fast-walked to the exit, since runners got detention. Once outside, she didn't see her friends; oh well, she would catch up on her cell later. At the second crosswalk, her plans came to a wrecking ball halt.

It was too good to be true; standing on the corner was that judge, Mr. Eastbrook. He called out quietly.

"Hi Tiffany, you mom asked me to tell you… there's a special makeup class at Avalon's. She's still at work but she'll meet you if you can get there… *somehow.*"

He turned and started walking away. Playing hard to get worked every time. The quick-thinking preteen caught up to him fast.

"A*re you going there*? Could give me a ride?"
He glanced at his watch, hesitating.
"Oh, well, I *SUPPOSE I could...* are you *READY?*"

The hesitation move was his pet move. Actually, he stole it from Ed Kemper, who had used it to great effect, killing coed after coed. The glance implied he was too busy to mess with little girls; a deal clincher.

"Yes, I'm ready right now!"
She fell in tow, three paces behind her killer. A man with a young girl trailing behind; nothing suspicious about it. He got in the Winnemako first and opened the valve on the Nitrous tank. Tiffany walked in and

looked at all the pretty things. Then the mask found her face; she went to sleep. She never felt the duct tape.

He caught the onramp, setting the cruise for 66, perfect for blending in Friday afternoon traffic; not too slow or too fast to attract troopers. There were plenty of speeding commuters to pull that duty. But in his near-orgasmic heat of the abduction, he forgot to plant forensics at Sandoval's. Normally he was methodical, but the super-sweet moments sometimes altered his plan. He doubled back to incriminate Sandoval; that asshole was a real pervert.

He drove home and parked; he had two hours until Sandoval would be unconscious. He eyed the pretty young lass, slumbering. He used tape to lift threads. Then he pulled six long blond hairs, roots and all. He nicked her left earlobe, swabbing blood with cotton-tipped swabs. Her blood tasted like copper. Putting the trace in ziploc bags, Eastbrook booted the cameras, locked up and went inside to wait in style.

He cooked pasta primavera, artichoke hearts and asparagus spears. Finishing the meal with just one glass of Hopland's premiere Zinfandel, careful not to overindulge. After he cleaned up, it was time to implicate Sandoval. The commuter rush was over, most neighbors closed their automatic garage doors and retired to couches. It would be another hour before joggers and triathletes hit the sidewalks.

Sandoval's was the last house in the cul de sac. It bordered a small brushy area, not really big enough to be a park. Actually it was leftover square footage left fallow, due to some endangered critter. They couldn't develop it and they couldn't sell it, so Sandoval got it with his house. the bushy lot appealed to his wild side.

David walked along, blending like experts always do. His shoulders slumped, strides smaller than normal; he wasn't going anywhere important... too boring to catch or hold attention.

Sandoval's old Biscayne waited patiently; its forty-year-old paint surrendered decades ago to the relentless sun... a mosaic of tiny paint spots isolated by rust moats.

Long ago, somebody lost the keys. No matter; a man could twist the ignition wings and the engine would light. As for the trunk, its first owner took his date out for a night of drinking and hopefully, screwing. But the punk left his keys in the supermarket, too absorbed with fake ID and beer. They got to the makeout point, a pal had an ax; beer and sex abounded.

It was way before bungie cords were invented, so bailing wire secured the trunk, which was more expedient than keys. When it came to beer, one could never be too careful.

The Biscayne's front and back seats were big enough for comfortable screwing, a fact not lost on teens of the era; they'd go on 'double dates', preserving parental illusions of propriety while allowing two sets of naked butts to simultaneously have their ease. But teens inevitably become adults and their vices do, too; far easier to drink and fuck at home. So the sun-faded, screwed-out, trunk-hacked Chevy got traded for a station wagon.

Eastbrook noticed the hacked trunk on his first recon trip; a sun-faded Bungie tethered the trunk, its topside worn-through to gray rubber strands, most of which were already busted.

He quickly worked the evidence out with his latex gloves. He dropped them through the rear window, where they landed on the seat. Kneeling down, he wiped the bloody swabs on the seat. Not enough to be obvious, but sufficient for luminol and DNA typing.

Time is paradoxical; ten seconds would give Sandoval ten decades in prison later. It felt like foreplay to know it would facilitate Eastbrook's continued predation. Sandoval would awaken to see splinters of pine molding flying while officers drew guns, every trigger finger itching for the pervert to twitch so they could waste his worthless ass.

Next would be the interrogation, aimed at incriminating, not justice. It was cop foreplay; something to do until the main course served up forensics. Once they had fibers and blood, the goose was cooked. Juries love their DNA, even when it lies.

Properly staged trace could easily bring a wrongful conviction, especially for a Sandoval; nobody would believe he was framed, but even if they did, they wouldn't care. A man like Sandoval had no chance for a fair trial.

A man has the right to counsel, but the poorer the accused, the less importance this right holds. The poor get a state-sponsored advocate; overloaded with cases, the low-budgeted PD's goal is to convince the accused to take a plea. To get an acquittal would take the type of lawyer Sandoval could never afford, but no such hero was on the horizon.

Eastbrook was glad he was rich. If he ever needed, he could buy the best counsel on earth. He got home in time for his favorite TV gameshow. Too bad that letter-turning woman was so old. He watched the show and fantasized that she had a young daughter.

TORTURE

In the semi-dark RV, Tiffany awoke, vacillating between abject horror and the desperate, delusional optimism of youth when death is imminent. Her psyche grappled with the duality; here was a man she knew, a judge, civic leader. And yet the look in his eyes hadn't been soft and convivial. It was the look of a viper before it strikes. The key turning the lock busted her thoughts.

A small puddle of urine indicated that one bodily need had been met while she was out. Her piss smelled sweet. His penis hardened, but he fought off the urge to just fuck the shit out of her right then.

Her eyes cleared; the judge's face slowly came into focus. She tried to speak but the gag banned it.
"Oh, so what do we have here… a little *starlet?*"

Her frightened eyes spurred his lust; it always did, to see her so purely frightened. With a flick of his knife, he slit the tape. He inserted a straw and offered the mark a bottle of water.
"I know how thirsty you must be… *TIFFANY,* isn't it?"

In spite of her fear; she drank the bottle empty, without breathing. The urge to survive is nowhere as strong as in a young child. She took a big breath.
"Why are you doing this to me?"

The duct tape garbled the words, but he knew the questions, always the same… *why are you doing this, please let me go,* and *please don't hurt me.'* That one really turned him on. Feeling his erection building, he lusted to scare her more.

"I'm doing this because… *I CAN.* You're the minnow. I'm the shark. Next question, please."

She went cold. Her mind raced.

"*PLEASE* let me go…"

"OH, I am afraid I can't; *You're MINE!*"

Then it hit her; she really was going to die; she hit the third query right on cue.

"Please don't hurt me!"

That third plea busted his initial plan; the look in her eyes triggered him. His left hand went up her thigh while his right hand rubbed his penis. Tiffany tried to roll out of his vice-like grip. His eyes glazed and he hissed at her.

"Shhhh… be a good little girl… give Davey what he wants and Davey won't… *HOLD STILL!* Let me touch it, and I won't kill your parents. *I like* killing parents!"

Up until then, the mark only thought of herself. Now the danger spread to her family; she became paralyzed with fear as the hand crept spider-like toward her vagina. She squeezed her eyes shut and whimpered. There was nothing else to do; she couldn't scream loud enough. She couldn't fight. She tried to wiggle but that just turned him on. She was totally fucked… or so she thought.

To children, things never seem like they can get worse. Tiffany learned how ineffective that school abduction film really was. The hand touched her privates, then it retracted. She opened her eyes to see her first adult penis; ugly, crooked and swollen. Just then, some liquid spurted out and the pervert moaned; "Oh, Margaret… you filthy bitch…"

The reddish brown penis shrank. He quickly stuffed it in his pants. The viper's death stare was gone. In its place was contempt, hatred or something she'd never seen before; after all, she was young.

He brought out a hunting knife, long, sharp and shiny. She shuddered. He cut the tape on her ankles, retaping them much wider. He cut her panties right up the middle. In an agonizingly ritualized movement, he removed the underwear and wiped it across his face; the matador's red blanket. He savored her terror, while her naked vulva lay trembling and helpless. Just as he'd hoped, no hair down there; she was perfect.

His fingers breached her vagina; fiery pains shattered her psyche. She cried out, but it spurred him on. Now three fingers probed and tore at her. Gone was his childlike voice, replaced with guttural, bestial groaning. His left hand ripped at her while his right stroked, timing it with her screams. Twin strands of drool dribbled from the corners of his mouth, spilling onto her chest. Eastbrook was in the zone.

The more blood and fear he saw, the harder he hand-fucked her and stroked his twisted old dick. With each breath she drew, Tiffany screamed as loudly as possible, even though it turned him on; her pain was too intense to keep inside.

She felt the long filthy fingernails ripping her insides. Hot blood poured down her ass crack. Metallic adrenaline emanated from pervert and victim. Eastbrook kept his bestial chant; *"You bitch… you tattle… you like it when I jerk off? I'll jerk off… on you, you filthy bitch"*

He was in the zone all right, the time zone; four decades in the past. It was always the same…

The girl went limp, sensory overload finally forcing her

unconscious, paradoxically bringing Eastbrook out of his trance. It wasn't any fun without bleeding and pleading. He went flaccid, his eyes cleared.

Whenever he came out of the memories, he felt sick and ashamed. Fortunately, he knew how to get past that. He tossed cold water on her. Her eyes opened, but the mark wasn't responding. She had experienced enough fear and pain for twenty lifetimes. Tiffany was gone away, to a dark place; there was a new personality. Had she lived longer, it would've earned a name.

Eastbrook was puzzled and frustrated; the tattletale bitch wouldn't play. He hadn't even got to the good part yet, with his drawer of rape tools. He tried slapping her, but no dice. He pinched her all over, but that didn't work either.

Opening the drawer, he went for his favorite tool, the tapered plastic vacuum nozzle. Maybe that would scare her back to him. Sticking it into her anus, he was slightly aroused. He shoved it in harder; only a slight reptilian grunt came, but it was enough to trigger Eastbrook; he found himself breaking another rule; he rammed his penis into her. It was surprisingly, wonderfully lubricated with hot blood. He spouted what little semen he had left.

He rolled off the broken child, slowly coming to his senses. Apparently, a long time passed while he was in the zone. Soon he felt contempt, because he broke his cardinal rule about DNA in victims.

He was in trouble, parked next to his home. Someone *HAD* to be looking for the bitch by now. And yet, as the tension of the situation hit him, he found it erotic. A new spice to an old game; he vowed to prolong it.

He tried to get her conscious. He closed his left hand around the tiny neck, just enough to arrest the airflow. After forty seconds, the body squirmed and the eyes bulged. He saw clarity return to her eyes. He let go. The girl sucked in a massive breath. It was reverse CPR, but it worked. Tiffany was back, and better still, she was pleading and squirming more than ever; nothing like primal strangulation to exorcise multiple personalities.

Somehow the mouth tape got loose; maybe it was the nearly comatose relaxation of her facial muscles, sweat, tears or whatever, but… She sucked air to scream for help, but no scream came out; it was her worst childhood nightmare. The boogeyman had her.

He saw her lungs expand; one scream could spoil the whole show. He squeezed, crushing her pharynx like an eggshell. Secondary muscles of respiration labored to lift the thorax for air. Meanwhile, her diaphragm heaved spasmodically upon the lower ribs; anything to get air. But no air came through the crushed pharynx.

He liked watching her writhe and gasp for air. He wanted to be inside her while she was suffocating. He tried to mount her but his penis wasn't up to it. That pissed him off.

He rubbed his shit-covered genitalia all over her loins, trying to will his member into service. Her scent wafted into his nose and throat; he could damned near eat her. He clenched down on her tiny throat, the throat that scorned him and tattled on him so many years ago. Then she died.

He went to the shower. It was time for re-entry. A man had to have a perfect re-entry, after a busted orbit like this one. He donned clean clothes and walked past the body on his way to the RV kitchen.

He poured a nice Merlot. He needed to get calm, because he broke his rule about depositing semen in the tattletale bitch.

From his darkened perch in the RV, the killer calmly studied the passing squad car. Its emergency lights weren't flashing, so it was probably responding to the nervous parent's call. He sipped and kept planning.

He discarded the impulse to dump it at Sandoval's, since his DNA in her ass would spoil the frame-up. He could burn it. This was not to his liking, although he did crave a good fire now and then. Fires generate attention, which was bad for a serial killer's survival.

He could pour gasoline into the anus. It sounded fun, but Eastbrook had little interest in orifices, once they stopped writhing. That left option three; depositing the body in a remote place where scavengers would eat up all traces; since this was his original plan, he went with it.

Polishing off the Merlot, he dumped the body in the freezer; it would take at least a day and a half before the inner organs were frozen solid. He would use that time wisely, planning every minor detail. By the time the mark was a Popsicle, he'd have it planned perfectly. He booted security cameras, locked the rig and carried the laundry inside his garage.

He pulled the vacuum cleaner bag. That and the baggies of fibers and bloody swabs went into a trash bag, along with his laundered sheets and blankets. He drove twenty miles to a Dumpster; homeless people would have the blankets by morning. Soon they would sport new semen and fibers. The pervert got home for the news at midnight. He would rest until dawn, before taking his road trip.

Life was good.

ANXIETY

Divorced for six years from a worthless deadbeat ex-husband, it fell on Jennifer to rear her daughter. Determined to give Tiffany a better life, she worked weekdays in graphic arts and weekends as a cocktail waitress, to keep Tiffany supplied with the tools to become a future star.

There were plenty of open palms; choreographers, trainers, beauticians, music lessons and pageant fees. Still, Shelly thrived in competition; and now that she had Avalon's attention, shel was a shoe-in for TV spots. Avalon's placed eighty percent of their clients. Of course they charged a lot. But, as their agent said; "Avalon's doesn't cost... *it pays.*"

She had less than an hour to get home, kiss her kid and haul ass to the "Pick O' the West", the area's last free standing honky-tonk. Thanks to urban sprawl, The Pick's days were numbered, but for the time being, rednecks and urban cowboys congealed there every weekend.

She came home to an empty house, but that wasn't unusual. Shelly usually stayed at a friend's rather than come home to the emptiness. Jennifer took a quick shower and donned her uniform. Passing the answer machine, she got nervous when it wasn't blinking. That wasn't like Shelly; she always left a message.

A small knot started forming. Anxious mothers know the knot, and no matter what... the fucking knot just grows. Worse yet, it is almost always right.

She dialed Shelly's cell. Ten seconds later the phone rang, sitting in its charger in her bedroom. Shelly never went anywhere without it, so she hadn't been home yet. The knot grew some more.

It only took ten minutes to learn Shelly wasn't with *ANY* of her friends. Her next call went to the Pick. Howard growled, but it was just window dressing. He loved Jen and her kid. He put her fears to rest.

"Ah, take it easy, Jen, she's prob'ly getting a pizza, kissin' a beau or somethin' and forgot her phone... call me when you know somethin', huh?"

Her next call went to 911. Dispatch took in the data. They'd send a unit immediately. The car arrived twenty minutes later; not bad, for a city so large.

Officer Sue Miller wasted no time.
"Good evening, Ma'am; Officer Susan Miller, Gander City PD... I understand your daughter didn't come home today, is that correct?"

Her knees wobbled; the sight of a uniform drove the message home... she had a real-world problem; denial, anxiety and hope vied for dominance.

"I checked *everywhere*; I don't know what to do!"

Miller handled a dozen lost kid calls a week; it was usually booze, dope, love or all the above. Or custody issues; one ex took the kid and forgot to mention it.

Still, parents always wanted an air search, FBI and every available unit. The *LAST* thing any nervous parent wanted was to think their kid was up to no good. Miller didn't shrink from her duty.

"Does your daughter have a boyfriend?"

"No… she's barely ten!"

Miller bit her tongue; she'd seen ten year-olds pregnant, hooked on drugs, even commit murder or suicide. She hit the next hot button.

"Does she drink or do drugs, to your knowledge?"

Jennifer gasped and exploded in exasperation.

 "*NO!* She's a normal kid! We're wasting TIME Officer, please help find her!"

"Mrs. Simpson, I do this all the time. I know it's hard, but please answer my questions… Trust me; *this is the fastest way!* Try to control yourself."

"I'm sorry… I'll try."

"Do you have a recent photograph or two? Her hairbrush, toothbrush… that would be helpful."

Jennifer went cold; she'd seen this on TV, but it held more gravity now that it was HER kid in the mix. She ran into the house for pictures while Miller keyed her mike and floated the data into the airways.

"Caucasian female, long blonde, blue, ten years, slight build, five one, 85, birthmark low back. white skirt, pink top, Last seen 15:30, 5700 San Simeon"

Dealing with distraught parents was tough enough, without them hearing the vic's particulars going onto the airwaves. Finishing up, she saw the vic's mother bringing photographs and a cell phone.

"These are recent photos and here's Shelly's cell phone; I think she's got a few self-shots on it."

Studio glossies; so the kid was a future star, but then, in L.A., *weren't they all?* The officer's guts tightened; this kid was a goner. Still, she stuck to protocol.

"Mrs. Simpson, could she be with your ex husband… or a boyfriend *of yours* perhaps?"

Miller scrolled through the kid's cell phone pictures, her mind idling while waiting for an answer; the vic's mother got pissed, ranted about working two jobs, no time for men, yes her ex was a deadbeat asshole, years behind in child support, but he wouldn't take Shelly; hell, he never even called her.

The cop saw the big picture; this kid was ripe for stealing. She bagged the items.

"Well, stay home and stay off your phone. I'll call if I hear *ANYTHING*, ok?"

She headed off to pick up her partner, Steve Warner, before responding to the next call; some asshole beating his wife. Speaking of assholes, she hoped he had his pants back on by now. She was tired of covering for him. Besides, he'd been banging that hooker for an hour already. She never could see what he saw in those cheap hookers.

Jennifer watched the squad car drive off into the darkness. Somewhere out there, her baby was in the dark. She couldn't go to work now. The urban cowboys would have to grope another waitress tonight.

Her next call was to her mother. In spite of the cop's admonition to keep the lines open, she just had to talk to her mother. After that, she sat on the couch and wailed while the reality sunk deeper; Shelly wasn't at a friend's, at the mall, kissing a boy or getting drunk. She was gone; the hours dragged on.

SUSPICION

Kylee Lacier hurried the particulars to command post for missing children, simultaneously broadcasting; "All units, BOLO missing Caucasian female, approximately ten years, shoulder length blond, blue, five one, 85, pink blouse, white skirt... last seen, 57 block San Simeon, 15:30"

Forty-five squad cars would be on the lookout. It was a surprisingly effective search system, in spite of the fact that they received plenty of such calls every month.

But they would definitely be on the lookout for *this one*; the long arm of the law always got a bit longer whenever the vic was a pretty Caucasian... She was on the Amber Alerts within ten minutes. Of course, the huge electronic billboards on major traffic arteries wouldn't help *this case*. They usally said things like; *"Stolen child, red Ford Pickup truck, LIC# ADC 778... last seen north on I 15."*

But Shelly was a cookie-cutter Barbie, in Southern Cal. Two hundred thousand motorists per hour passed the Alerts and yawned; until they described the perp, vehicle or some distinguishing characteristic, the alerts were useless. But even so, the signs were out there.

Tim Dockins told his officers just as much, during the shift briefing.
"Ok, guys... this one's *HOT*. We got a girl missing; CAUCASIAN, ten, blond, blue, last seen JFK Elementary, wearing pink, white."

"Burkey, Gonzales, take the local perverts, a mile radius to start; odds are good we'll net the perp right there. Blisters, Jalapeno, check her hangouts. Maybe she's puffin' a joint. I know, she's only ten, but where have we heard *that* before?"

Half the cops nodded.

"Miller took the prelim, so if you get a lead, shoot it to her, too. Let's get her home tonight! Go to work and be sure to come home alive."

Fifteen minutes later, Lister and Jalapez parked at their first spot. At that hour, the mall was deserted. They showed the rent-a-cop a photo and got nothing. They left for the next hangout, an open storm drain where kids went to smoke dope.

They found six little bastards smoking Pot and chewing tobacco. They managed to collar two of them. Lister played bad cop; Burkey, good.

"You're under arrest; you have the right to remain..."
"Oh, wait a second, do we *really* need to bust 'em?"
Both pre-teens mutely shook heads in the negative.
Lister softened a bit; he showed the flier.
"Well, *MAYBE* I don't see the dope. You know her?"
The short kid found his voice first.
"I think that's Shelly Simpson. DUDE... *Is she dead?*"
"I'll ask the questions... so you know her?"

Biff shrugged.
"Not really; too young, dude, and she don't smoke."
They scared the boys and let them go. The pot smelled too good for Lister to let it go to waste on the punks. He wondered how they could afford such good shit. Jalapez didn't smoke, but he didn't give a shit if his partner did... After work. They drove off.

"Well she don't hang at the mall or with the druggies. Let's try the small strip mall between school 'n home; maybe she stops for candy or what, eh?"

And so it went. By the end of their shift, Lister capped their work with one profound statement.

"*THIS kid's*... just fuckin' *gone!*"

But while Blisters and Jalapeno drew blanks, Burkey and Gonzalez hit pay dirt. It took just a few mouse clicks to get the shit on six local pedophiles living close to the Simpson residence. They went alphabetically.

Ronnie Lapique was recently released. His PO was helpful; yes, he got out three days ago. Yes, he was a dangerous predator, but he stalked minority boys, the darker the better. True, sometimes a predator will switch forage, but more to the point, he was already in custody for biting a young Hispanic boy on the coast. Actually, it was *on the ass* while *AT the coast,* but the bigger question was... how could he abduct a girl when he was already jailed?

Next were Mavis, Sandoval and Woods. Gonzales went to the door while Burkey went around back...no sounds, no vehicle and no body noise confirmed it. That placed Mavis high on the suspect list. They'd come back to him.

At Sandoval's place, Burkey hit the front door while his partner watched the back. Hispanic music blasted, but in between beats, they heard snoring. Gonzales left his post and peeked into Sandoval's car.

He thought he saw some blood on the rear seat or he wouldn't have probable cause. Then they beat down his door. Fuck the warrant; the pervert stole a kid... They didn't have time to fuck around.

They saw Sandoval on the couch, snoring like a chainsaw. No weapons, hands empty, half-empty bottle of whiskey sideways on coffee table. The pervert's stench was overpowering.

Burkey thumped him on the left shin with his baton. The asshole never twitched. Gonzales solved it with a saucepan of tap water. Sandoval came to, gurgling a mixture of water and stale vomit, the latter having spent the last hour between his cheek and gums.

His vision started to clear; two cop-blue images. He tried to get up, but the baton to his clavicle cured that impulse. In spite of the whisky buzz, it hurt like a bitch.
"Ow! Whatthefuck you do that for?"
Burkey cocked for another swing.
"That was to get your attention, chingado... you wanna 'nother... or you ready to talk, kiddy fucker?"
Sandoval couldn't recall molesting anyone lately. A few sobering neurons started firing.

"WHAYOUWANNAKNOW?"
"Where you been since three, you sick bastard?"
That was easy; he'd been home, drinking his ass off... the problem, as he already knew, was that it was no alibi whatsoever. He was cooked. He decided to try the truth.

"I been here, drinkin' and listenin' to my musica... See?"

He grandly waved an arm around, encompassing the stereo, bottle and not much more.

Gonzalez could easily test his statement.
"Bill, you want me to get the Breathalyzer?"

"No."
He didn't want the truth; he wanted a conviction.

"We got a guy with a rap sheet and no alibi. Squawk it in… we need a forensics crew, right now."

They cuffed the bastard and put him into the unit, being careful to bang his head several times on the squad car roof. Considering his bigger problems, it's doubtful Sandoval noticed.

FORENSICS

Sarah Blacklock hated molesters with a vengeance, since she had been a victim at thirteen; if she had her way, every pedophile would die a slow, agonizing death. Preferably due to dildo.

Her partner Bill Dunn was a plodding cop with a monastic obsession. Many times his peers gave up, rubbing their necks in fatigue, while Dunn kept plodding. He was a boring duplex, with no curbside appeal; the kind of man most women automatically overlook, but he was all about the job.

They sped through the neighborhood, eager to get to the perp's residence. Sarah took the residence while Dunn went straight for the vehicles; the battered jeep in the garage could wait. The Biscayne on the street couldn't.

The bathroom J-trap was a gold mine. Blacklock was soon up to her ears in hair and fibers. Most of it appeared to belong to the perp, with a few appearing to be Negroid, but nothing blond; so he hadn't brought waspy girls into this shithole.

Her partner whistled outside, so she hurried out. Dunn stood by the Chevy, grinning and holding a strand of hair like a trophy wildebeest. They cordoned off the scene and called for a uniform to guard it, then they raced to the lab. The DNA testing results would take longer, but so far, it was almost a lock. That, plus the rare blood type; AB negative. It matched Simpson's type. It looked bad for Greasy Chris.

INTERROGATION

Crystobal Arnolfo Sandoval sat in the cinderblock interrogation room, resigned to his fate. His head ached. These last cops were relatively light-handed; softer than his last bust in Bakersville; it took six weeks in the hospital to recover from that interrogation. He put his head down on the cool steel tabletop; it felt good against the fresh contusions.

Lieutenant Medaris entered, eager to gut the bastard. The rotting-fruit stench from the chronic alcoholic slammed him like a six-foot curl; he wished he were surfing, with the cool ocean air blasting him, instead of this sick kiddy fucker's Keto-acidotic stench. He slammed the door for intimidation.

Sandoval twitched bolt upright, revealing a freshly battered face. Medaris knew the source; Sandoval escaped the squad car. Then he probably fell face first, with hands cuffed behind his back; he sparred with the arresting officers. Those child-raping bastards always resisted; in spite of both officers being fully trained in non-lethal force; taser, beanbags and tear gas, the perverts always got knuckles, boots and batons; just another those law enforcement mysteries. Call it Blue Physics.

Greasy Chris went five six, 125, yet he chose to duke it out with two officers, each outweighing him two to one; at any rate, Medaris would buy 'em drinks later. His current focus was razor-sharp and singular... Obtain a confession at all costs. He sat down and signaled the mirrored glass to turn on the camera.

"Crystobal Sandoval, MY NAME is Lieutenant John Medaris. I'm here to ask you about the abduction of Tiffany M. Simpson; you wanna save us both some time, and confess right now?"

Oddly enough, some of 'em actually wanted to confess, shortly after being beaten. Some lacked impulse control, making Medaris' query more effective than most civilians might imagine. Sandoval, however, just shrugged. He couldn't understand the words; they sounded blurry. His headache kept getting worse.

"You DO know your rights, don't you?"

Again, with the noncommittal shrug. Medaris gave him the Miranda speech again, just to get it on record. Sandoval caught the gist, purely from the cadence. Cops always read it with the same rhythm.

"You have the right to remain silent. Anything you say... blah, blah... same shit, different precinct... Only this time, the words grew more garbled; the room swirled. Just as Medaris finished his speech, Sandoval's face hit the steel tabletop.

Fortunately for the video record, it wasn't a cop's fist slamming the suspect's face. It was the subdural hematoma putting pressure on his brainstem; Greasy Chris checked out... He was finally cured.

Nobody was happy. Medaris had a missing kid. His only lead just died. Jalapez and Lister would be investigated for allegedly killing the suspect.

And certainly if he knew of it, Eastbrook wouldn't be happy. Gone was his scapegoat, so perfectly framed that Sandoval would never have gotten free. Well, the sonofabitch was free now... as free as death permits.

FALLOUT

It would be hard to get the troops to do an about face and look for other suspects, because Sandoval looked too good for this one. The case would center upon finding the girl or her body; and for that there seemed to be no finer place to start than Sandoval's residence.

By morning, cops completed searching house and adjoining brushy lot, knowing how some perverts love bushy hiding places. The first pass consisted of twenty-five officers abreast, barely two yards apart. They found nothing to incriminate him in the Simpson case, but they did find several articles of clothing, which belonged to missing Hispanic boys.

By afternoon the second search started, consisting of SAR members, schoolteachers, parishioners and firefighters; there seemed no end of good people willing to help. At five thirty, Eastbrook answered a knock on his door. A bony woman of twenty-two held up the flier.

"Hi; we're trying to locate Tiffany; have you seen her?" Eastbrook eyed the photo of his newest victim. Fighting back drool, he just shook his head. The tired woman didn't notice as she handed him a flier.
"Well, please keep an eye out. Thank you."

The busy-bee do-gooder buzzed off, pollinating each house on the west side of the street, while her partner draped the east.

He had a dead body just fifteen yards from the very people that wanted it, and the morons didn't suspect a thing. It lit a fire in his guts. He toyed with the notion of sticking around to watch the fools fail. They were so stupid... they'd never catch him.

The bloodhounds came just before dusk, while he watered his lawn. Their leashes strained tight; they were eager to be out of their kennel. Maybe the scent they sought was just ahead. They couldn't be sure, because they were just dogs... Townsend got within half a block before he waved and hailed.

"HEY, PASTOR EASTBROOK! HOW'S IT GOIN'?"

Normally he wasn't given to recalling young men, but the voice gave the kid away. He had a signature whine, an annoying inflection, making every statement sound like a question. Eastbrook tried to think; Townsend, maybe. Yeah, that was it; Darien... no, *Darwin*... that was it.

He waved and smiled, as he shit a brick about the bloodhounds; they'd be there in ten seconds. Knowing they might scent the body, he did the only thing that might save his child-raping ass. He walked to the RV, so when the dogs got there, curious sniffing might be overlooked. His fear was almost paralyzing.

The bloodhounds pulled him every step of the way. When they hit Eastbrook's lawn and Townsend stopped, they started looking for a place to piss. The handler paid no mind; he was enamored with the ex-pastor, business-genius, and owner of a huge fantasy-based role-playing software company. Darwin rushed to shake Eastbrook's outstretched hand.

"Good to see you, Pastor?"

The pervert raised his left hand in mock objection, while the outstretched right hand readied to give him the Pope's handshake.

"Oh, nobody calls me *'Pastor'* anymore, Darwin… call me *DAVE*… and my, what fine dogs you've got there!"

He knelt and rubbed his face in theirs, hoping cologne would overload olfaction. They sniffed and licked but his scent wasn't what they sought. He stood up and put on his baby-stealing face.
"AWFULLY good to see you again, son! What brings you to this neighborhood?"

Townsend's answer formed as the hounds sniffed the killer's crotch. He pretended not to look.

"I'm volunteering for the Simpson search?… But my dog Honey's at the vet's?… So I borrowed Beau and Duke from a really close friend? *She* couldn't get time off, so *she* loaned 'em to me?"

He emphasized the *she,* hoping Eastbrook would be impressed. It wasn't every day he got a girl's attention, especially a hottie like Kaylee Parker. But he didn't take the hint, so Townsend hit the gender clue harder.

"They're great dogs, and *SHE* trained 'em well, but I'm not used to 'em? Bloodhounds are different than my Golden, that's for sure?"

Almost on cue, Beau sniffed the RV drainpipe; it smelled almost exactly like the sock from the mark's hamper. The hound refreshed his memory of the sample scent; relaxed, ate pepperoni and chocolate, just hours before removing the socks; and she wasn't pregnant or in heat.

But the scent emanating from the RV smelled different; she was afraid before dying; ate a ham sandwich and milk four hours before dying... heavy traces of adrenaline, fear and urine. Still, the base scent belonged to the mark. He made a low whoof... That was his job.

Perhaps if Townsend were more familiar with the hounds, it would've sealed Eastbrook's fate. Instead, he just jerked the leash and pulled the dog off point. Eastbrook felt his rectum spasm, but he adapted fast.

"Well, they must like fish, because last weekend I cleaned a stringer of bass in my sink; could they actually smell those fish, Darien?"

Darwin was eager to impress his hero.
"Uh, *it's Darwin?* Oh, yeah, these hounds have incredible noses? They can sniff out three parts per million? Give him the right conditions, Pasto... I mean... *Dave,* and they can probably tell what the fish were eating when you caught 'em?"

Eastbrook feigned amazement, raising eyebrows, lifting chin; the only motion he could make, which might conceal his terror.
"*AMAZING!*
"Yeah?"
"Are you having any luck with the search?"
"No, they caught the perp, but he died last night during questioning? He had a heart attack? Anyhow, we're just cold trailing, hoping to find the body, I mean Shelly Simpson? Anyhow, I better get to it, Pastor... I mean *Dave,* maybe I'll see you at church tomorrow?"

The killer could barely manage a nod.
"Sure... Oh, I forgot; I have to drive to Las Vegas tomorrow. Maybe next week."
"Well, see you then?"
"Yes, maybe so."

The ass-kisser headed down the street, pulling two perplexed hounds. Luckily for Eastbrook, the fresher Simpson scent drifted up through the roof vent pipe, into the blowing crosswind; Lord bless those late afternoon winds. The rapist had a sudden urge to crap, so he scurried into the house. He almost made it to the toilet before he soiled his pants.

As he cleaned up he pondered the bloodhounds. Had the dog *really* smelled the tiniest of molecules through the mixture of detergent, gray water and bleach? Perhaps that was why it didn't do a full point.

Two things saved him; Townsend's unfamiliarity with the hounds, and his infatuation with Eastbrook… Denial is the patron saint of perverts; NOBODY cleans fish in a high-end RV.

The close call had him feeling the lethal injection needle. Without Greasy Chris for a scapegoat, it was anyone's guess where the investigation might lead. He fired up the Winnemako; time to get the hell out of Dodge.

Driving one block upwind of the searching hounds, he turned left on Sepulveda and headed for the freeway. Two streets over, both Beau and Duke wailed when the fresh scent temporarily wafted. For just a moment, the new handler thought he had a lead, but then they resumed cold trailing; they were probably sniffing some hot bitch in a nearby backyard.

It was the last time they pointed any leads for the strange handler. What was the use? The dogs knew a rookie when they had one on the leash.

RE-ENTRY

Setting the cruise for an honest 63 per, the Winnemako blended with right-lane northbound, irritating folks behind him. That made a perfect cover; just another rude, arrogant RV prick. More than a few gave him the finger when they passed his fat ass.

By the time he hit the Grapevine, he had his nerve back. His plan was to rent a jeep in Bakersville and head into the desert. Ninety minutes later he parked on the outskirt of the lot, locked up and went into the building. Soon a gopher had the Jeep hooked to the back of his rig. He hauled ass for the desert.

Eastbrook intended to idle the big RV into the desert a few miles, where he wouldn't be seen dragging the stiff into the Jeep. But his plan wasn't so great, as he soon discovered. The first wave of dirt bikes passed, kicking dust and rocks on their way to some rally. When the second wave passed him, he got the hint; he needed a lonelier spot. He hit the interstate and headed north.

Gradually, traffic thinned out. The south Sacramento Valley held little of interest; an unending expanse of dry, brown earth and played-out oil wells, each with their dead ant-like pump standing guard. Then the terrain started to improve, giving way to nut orchards, hayfields, stockyards and of course the canal; a long artery of life, flowing down the concrete trough from the Delta in the north, all the way down the valley. He toyed with dropping the body in the canal, but feared it would be found too soon.

The expanse of orchards held the same risk; there had to be workers tending them. He hit Sacramento six hours later, just when he ruled out Nevada. He was unfamiliar with northern Nevada. Southern Nevada, he knew that like the back of his perverted dick. He kept heading north.

Finally he made his selection as he refueled the behemoth gas-guzzler.

He had been to Mendonesia County before. It was a poor county but held diverse attractions; spring brought abalone divers and wine tours. Summer saw boaters, anglers and sightseers. Autumn hosted deer hunters, pot buyers and itinerant harvesters for its crops, both legal and otherwise. Winter drew steelhead anglers and mushroom hunters, if the rains were good.

His first visit to the North Coast was five years ago, to buy varietal wines; an excellent piece of camouflage since most people associated high cuisine with high ethics... a major flaw in thinking, but a common one, so rich pedophiles always exploited it.

He surfed a down-looking satellite website. He selected a perfect piece of BLM land; plenty of steep, forested terrain, the faintest trace of an unimproved road, greenery, obviously a wintertime upload. He felt confident the two-track was used mainly during deer season. By the time any hunter happened upon it, the soft tissues would be consumed. He steered toward the summits, 70 miles to the northwest. The sun set behind the mountains before he saw a wooden sign.

"You are now entering Five Rivers National Forest. Be FIRE SAFE."

CYCLES

He found an unimproved campground; a typical flat spot at the base of some really wicked mountain passes, the last flat spot for fifty miles and six hours of four-wheeling. From the valley floor at 400 feet, the steep-ass winding road would summit, 17 miles and five thousand feet ASL.

After booting his security system, he turned to his evening meal; pasta primavera, with a heavy grating of Romano. Topping it off with a glass of Gewürztraminer, he hit the pillow early. He had it all; full belly, soft bed, frozen body to dump. His last conscious impressions were of a man snoring, far away. The first dream was good. The second dream, always the same, was bad.

"Hold STILL, DAVIE… HOLD STILL!" To reinforce the imperative, Millie struck him on the scalp with the spring-steel spatula. A scalpel thin line of red appeared when the weapon retracted for the next blow. Seeing the blood, Millie stopped; she didn't mean to harm the boy, just make him obey. It took God knows how many baths and spankings to keep the filthy lad on the straight and narrow.

She had been bathing him forever, but now that he was eleven; it seemed creepy. He shut his eyes. The coarse, soapy rag scratched like steel wool. Then her naked hand lathered it up; she would peel back his foreskin, soap up his tiny glans penis and scrub it raw with the washcloth.

Her lips silently formed the same word every time. On this bath, he finally figured out what the word was; her upper lip raised, exposing two front teeth like an angry rat, the tongue touched teeth for the second syllable. Suddenly the burning pain in his scalp left; surprisingly, the sensation became erotic. The tiny penis began to engorge involuntarily until the boy's first-ever erection brought her voice up to full volume… "filthy, Filthy, FILTHY… *FILTHY!"*

Confused by new, colliding experiences, he did what most kids would; he held still and watched; her eyes glazed over. She kept striking him.

She saw back to when her father bathed her and banged her with his filthy dick. He bathed her every filthy Friday night, until she was seventeen and ran away… but deep inside, on some dark level, she still missed Filthy Fridays, and she hated him for that, too. She would teach the filthy bastard, once and for all…

Her gaze fixed on the boy's stiff little penis; here was another filthy cock, in a world of filthy cocks; she couldn't stop them all, but by God, she could stop *this one*. Down came the spatula, smiting the filthy little pink mushroom cap across the tip. The boy screamed and sat forward, protecting his shrinking, bleeding genitals. Each subsequent blow rang on his scalp, perfectly timed with her mantra; *"FILTHY".* He passed out around the fortieth "Filthy".

Eastbrook awoke from the nightmare, sat bolt upright, trying to protect his loins; the spring-steel spatula still rang in his ears. It was four in the morning. The RV was freezing cold. Knowing what the next part of his dream would bring, he tried to circumvent it with hard alcohol. He sat in the captain's chair and poured a tall one. He drank and sat back in the chair, eyes far-focusing into the darkness beyond the windshield. He took another slug and hoped the hooch would make it go away… But the engram was branded too deep. He began to snore; the images returned, as always…

Things changed after that; Millie never let the boy out of the basement, except for school. He took his meals down there. He slept down there. He lived down there, an outcast from his only remaining family. He never brought any friends home; he couldn't bear having peers learn of his bizarre situation.

They lived upstairs, in fresh air and light; he was locked down there, with two 50-watt bulbs to light and heat it. They ate, laughed, watched TV and read the Bible. He heard them through the floor, and knew their routine like his own. Theirs was a world of fun and challenge; his was only punishment and abandonment. If there were a better soil in which to cultivate a serial killer, it would be hard to imagine it.

As he grew, he wondered; what was it about his penis that caused such a reaction in his aunt? He began to play with it, and finally he found out about the power; he had his first ejaculation. The hot thrill in his guts overwhelmed him. He tried to get the stuff to spurt out again, but he had to wait for it to recharge.

By his thirteenth year, he had managed to sneak a few filthy magazines into the basement. He became obsessed with his penis. One evening, he was so absorbed in masturbating, he forgot about Peggy's routine. She opened the door to bring the boy's dinner, unprepared for what she saw. Davy stood at the base of the stairs, back to her, pants down.

His body was jerking. He was looking at pictures. Curious as any ten year-old can be, she shifted position to see why her cousin was twitching. Then she saw it; a long, brownish-red thing. Moaning, he started rubbing it faster. Peggy took a step down to get a better view; the step creaked... Just then, Davy reached climax and turned toward the noise, semen spewing straight up at Peggy on the stairway.

But instead of being ashamed, Davy transferred his lust; the presence of another living person heightened it. He wished his dick could grow all the way up, under that skirt. He spurted over and over, each new spasm bringing another shot of milky semen. He arched his neck and moaned a bestial sound. It lasted thirty seconds; Peggy never moved; youthful curiosity paralyzed her.

When it quit spurting, she dropped the food tray and whirled to run. Dishes clattered and food spilled. He hurried to put his penis away; the thing could not be undone. She could no more keep a secret than stop breathing. It was two days before Peggy tattled. By then, the monster growing in the basement thought he got away with it.

Millie grew enraged when she learned of the sinful incident. She vowed that the beatings would resume, only she carried a thick oak dowel, not a cheesy little spatula; the filthy bastard contaminated her daughter.

He was just like his father and his uncle Waylon; filthy bastards, all. She flew down the stairs, surprising the sleeping boy on his makeshift couch. Words spat from her mouth; he couldn't recognize them. Over and over, the club split his scalp, flooding his eyes with blood.

Then adrenaline kicked in. He was done taking pain; it was time to dish it out. His vision blurred to a primal crimson, one thought dominated; *SURVIVE!* Catching her wrists in one hand, he spun her onto the couch. Stealing the club was surprisingly easy; thanks to the adrenaline rush. He sat on her thighs. The first blow knocked her into a light stage of shock. He raised the club for another blow, but the look on her face made him stop... Millie whispered coarsely.

"Give me that FILTHY DICK, WAYLON!" She thrust her pelvis up and pulled the boy's hips down. In a heartbeat, she had the boy's dick in her grasp. In the three years since she last bathed him, she was surprised how much it had grown. She guided it into her, chanting...

"Filthy, *FILTHY* COCK! *SISSY WANTS IT!*"

The surprised teenager dropped the dowel. It was hot and wet inside her, and scary too... The only thing scarier was the look on her face. Her sky-blue eyes rolled back, she moaned nonstop. Her pelvis throbbed and rubbed against him.

"FUCK ME... STICK YOUR FILTHY *COCK IN ME! DO IT HARD! FUCK ME, WAYLON!*"

He came almost immediately, but not the usual river he spurted while masturbating. Confused by the bizarre mix of sensations, he withdrew and looked; she was hairy and nasty down there. It wasn't the manicured airbrushed magazine pussy he'd studied in the girly mags. She stunk, too. Her eyes smoked with hatred.

"You can't even *FUCK ME RIGHT!* YOU'RE NO MAN... YOU'RE A FUCKING *FAGGOT!*"

She laughed as he pulled his pants up, embarrassed and ashamed. She continued attacking, until he finally got pissed off and picked up the dowel. One hard blow to the side of her head shut her disgusting mouth. She went limp. He reached for a pillow to suffocate her. Then he heard a noise. His cousin stood on the stairs; the voyeuristic bitch watched the whole thing. A sick little smile hung on her rosy red lips; so... the little bitch ratted him out, only to watch him get beaten and raped. The filthy little slut enjoyed the whole show.

Peggy realized her danger, but too late. He was on her in a heartbeat. Knocking her down on the stairs, adrenaline and rage commingled. He ripped off her skirt and panties. Her vulva was totally unlike his aunt's… there was no hair down there. It was just a nude little cleft; he liked it. Her blond hair dangled down three stairs. Her sky blue eyes bored into the boy; she was in shock. Her mother lay on the couch, probably dead. There was nobody to protect her.

"Please don't hurt me. I won't tell… Why are you doing this to me?"

A serial rapist was born. He got erect again, only he missed her vagina, entering her anus. The squealing and pleading stimulated him like nothing else. He came like a rocket ship. When he pulled out, his dick was covered in the thin, watery shit of a truly terrified human being.

FINALLY it *WAS* a FILTHY dick, just like Millie always said. He waddled down the steps, pants around his ankles and climbed onto comatose Millie. He rubbed the shitty filth onto her hair down there. Then he marched up to the kitchen and ate like a death row inmate. The power intoxicated him. He hit the streets and never looked back.

Nobody reported the abuse; there were way too many skeletons in Millie's closet. The authorities didn't need to know that the twisting tornado of abuse had such a long tail. Waylon's father was abused. Predictably, he started raping his first daughter when she turned nine. He kept that tradition going, daughter after daughter, all the way down to Millie. It was only natural that she kept it up. And passed it on... For, what good is a family, without tradition?

Eastbrook awoke just before sunup; a cold puddle of ejaculate told the tale; he'd been ass-fucking his cousin again. Wiping up, he flushed away another filthy nightmare. The sun rose; bright rays catalyzed him into action. He selected two magnetic signs, from an array of six different sets; *"High Country Photography... David Hayes, prop."*

He went to the cargo bay for a huge ice chest, carried it to the bed, propping the lid open. Then he opened the freezer; instead of a Popsicle, he had a thawing corpse. Apparently the pilot light went out during the night... It would account for the freezing cold RV, if he ran out of propane. He test-poked the left forearm; the skin was thawed down an inch, maybe more.

He had been counting on the solid-freeze to tweak the time of death. To refreeze it would take another 48 hours, assuming the freezer wasn't broken. That would put him overdue for his alibi business trip, so he went with his gut. He decided to dump it as-is.

He pulled on the body, hearing cracking sounds when the ice released her. He tried to stuff it into the chest, but she was too long, so he cut through the suprapatellar tendons to make the legs flex. After what seemed like an eternity of hacking and slicing, he finally got both nearly-amputated legs genu-flexed enough to fit.

The killer booted his security cameras and headed up the forest road; he had full tank of gas, a packed lunch and digging tools. And, to make it look good, a case full of camera gear. It was a nice day for dumping bodies. He found the side road near the second of three summits. It wasn't much, just a berm, water bar and sign saying "M-72". A small icon prohibited Off Road Vehicle use. There wouldn't be any rangers or wardens patrolling for ORV abusers, until the hunters would arrive in a few weeks.

Slipping into low gear, he easily climbed the berm. The satellite pictures were old; the trail was overgrown with Doug Firs and Scotch Pines, replants after the last fire, six or seven years ago, judging from limb growth patterns. It took an hour to cover three miles, thanks to snaking through the replants.

He found a small landslide depression, dragged the cooler over and dispassionately tilted its contents out. Except for a few oozing strands of trailing slime, the Popsicle hit exactly as planned; face up, torso in the deep end.

The hardpan was extremely tough to dig. Before long, the fat pervert tired of trying to bust roots with the pinch bar and move hard dirt with just a shovel; the nude pelvis and face were exposed. Not seeing any reason to continue, he loaded up. Besides, leaving her that way made her look more like a filthy tattle-tail bitch.

Then in a rare display of conscience, he got a small blanket and draped it over those dead eyes. He got back in the Jeep and snaked through the trees. When the sun went below the summits, he was back in his RV. He ate his traditional post-re-entry meal; peanut butter and orange marmalade, glass of milk and a single cold chicken thigh… the same meal he'd eaten so many years earlier from his aunt's fridge.

Soon his rig labored up the western Sierras. He felt smug, but if he'd known that the body never completely froze, another emotion would have surfaced.. The first clue was the ease with which her knees bent; no Popsicle child would ever bend so easily. But he was a pedophile, not a coroner. He it Reno, got a room, great meal and a fine cognac. He'd head south in the morning.

ACCEPTANCE

With each passing hour, Jennifer Simpson's heart sank deeper. What began as mere inconvenience steadily morphed into life-changing dread. She shuddered at the grisly thoughts ripping at her sanity. She had seen enough cop shows to know; the outlook was grim.

She had seen it in the officer's eyes... Her eyes spoke words a cop's lips could never say. If a child weren't found within three hours, the kid was dead. Jennifer fought hard to force a river of ugly scenarios away, but it didn't help.

Maybe Shelly wasn't dead... maybe it was worse! Maybe slave traders smuggled her to some third-world sex ring, sold into slavery, to black men with blacker hearts. She'd heard that some countries cut clits off their women. She'd heard it all... and it eroded her crumbling mind.

Her friends and mother were of little help; no hand wringing or hugging could palliate; the kid was gone, and that was that. There was no ransom note. The worst conclusion steamrolled her; some pervert had her daughter. She never felt so helpless.

She dialed Miller's number for the hundredth time; still no news. She reached for the gin to deaden her pain. A half-bottle later she passed out, but the images remained, wobbly and distorted by alcohol. She saw body parts with worms crawling, bits of her daughter on fire... the images wouldn't stop.

She awoke to the sound of her puke splashing onto the coffee table. She felt like killing herself. Without Shelly, she didn't know what to do. She took two Valiums, washing them down with the rest of the gin, hoping to shut out the evil, but the night wore on, one lonely tick of the clock after another.

PROFILES

Sarah Blacklock poured her man another Chardonnay; it was supposed to be a romantic dinner; both agreed to not talk shop, but they had little else to talk about. So the silence just hung there, as cool wine touched hot, young lips.

Eric Sangreal had two passions. One was Sarah, the other his work. That was what attracted her to him; he loved catching criminals... *especially* perverts.

Ever since she had been molested, her life had one focus; catching and punishing evil, heartless bastards. But while her focus was narrow, he caught all types of criminals. Actually, he didn't catch, his information did.

Sitting there sipping their wine, they finally caved in to the temptation. Eric broke the silence.
"So, I'm sorry, but I've gotta say this; that Sandoval case? Something doesn't ring true."

She cringed as the unwanted image of the stinking pedophile B&E'd her mind; perp died in custody. There'd be an investigation. She didn't want to have to lie in court about *not having* this conversation. She always hated testilying. Seeing her reaction, Sangreal deflected her fears.

"No... Before they busted him, he didn't fit the profile."
"Who cares? One less child molester on the planet... *Works for me!*"

But she knew how Eric's mind worked. He built his opinions one brick at a time, each one solidly set before proceeding. Once mortared into place, it could wait for the next brick. She sipped and waited.

"Sure, Sandoval was a sick bastard; but he targeted boys, Blacks and Hispanics. We popped him for a white girl. It's *POSSIBLE*, but it's *NOT PROBABLE."* He reached for a cracker to clear his palate.

"A pervert's behavior is hard-wired. They *CAN'T change...* It's how we catch 'em. Most pedophiles have an image in their psyche; an uncle, priest , whatever. That image never changes. *I guess* what I am saying... I think the REAL PERP'S still out there."

She looked deep into those hazel eyes. She loved him. She respected his work, because she had been trained to trust forensics; eyewitnesses rarely saw what they claimed. Alibis and motives rose and fell with the tide, but forensics alone were immutable, without agenda. That's why she chose the field.

Yet now she had two sets of controverting facts, both solid. Nibbling a cracker, she juxtaposed them; intellectual transparencies, overlaid, held up and inspected for commonalities and contradictions.

"SO... We got a pervert that does minority boys *AND* we got Caucasian girl trace. What can we deduce?"

Eric watched his lover's mind work, wineglass high at arm's length, eyes rolled up, frowning thoughtfully. "So... *HOW DID* the trace evidence get there?" He took a shot. "Well, if I'm right... S*omeone else put it there."* "*The COPS planted it?* Possible, but where did they get the blood? Miller had a hairbrush, but *no blood. "*

"OK, if it *wasn't a cop*; *who else* would plant it?

Well according to *your theory,* whoever it is, he likes blond-haired, blue-eyed girls."

It was too weird, but there it was; evidence pointed at an unknown subject. Eric nodded, speaking softly.
"He *framed* Greasy Chris? He's a smart unsub."
He emptied the last of the bottle into both goblets.
"We have an intelligent, organized serial rapist."

Blacklock looked unsure. She was so smart, but sometimes he forgot she wasn't trained in profiling.
"You got your big three serials; arsonists, rapists and killers. You got your *disorganized*; they lack organizational skill and impulse control."

He drained the wine.
"Then you got your ORGANIZED *serials*; good social skills, *PLAN* their deeds, get better with each crime."

She felt the building buzz while Eric kept going.
"At the top of the heap are the *intelligent, organized, serial killers;* If we don't catch 'em early, they can get so good that they become impossible to catch. They keep killing until they quit, die or get jailed for some other crime; they may take their secret to the grave and the jailers never knew they were holding a serial killer."

Eric moved closer and put his arm around her.
"So, let's assume it's not the wine talking; we might be looking for just such an unsub... A senior family member or authority figure abused him. The victims bear a striking resemblance to the original abuser... If and when we catch them, it's often due to the physical similarities."
"Really?"
"Yep. He starts out early, maybe as a peeping tom, then stalker, then molester. Later he escalates to rape, raises the bar to torture and finally, killing. With

each kill, he gets better at everything. There are bells and whistles, but that's the gist of it. I give you; 'intelligent, organized serial rapist/killer, Lesson One."

But Sarah no longer listened; her mind was fifteen years into the past, trying to fight off her asshole stepfather. She pulled Eric close, trying to ward off the ugly images. It never worked, but it was worth a shot.

Eric knew the drill; he hugged her tight and shut his mouth. They went to bed. It was a sick fucking world out there, just outside their door.

In the morning, Sarah's first call went to her partner.
"Bill, did you finish the Sandoval evidence?"
Not even through his first coffee, Dunn grunted.
"Good morning to *you too*, sweetheart..."
He actually liked her get-to-the-point style, but he wanted to rib her; he knew she'd be squirming while waiting for the facts.
"Yah, pretty much finished."
"Did you find anything to suggest the evidence might have been planted?"
She never minced words. He liked that, too.
"Well, the hair was pulled out by the roots, consistent with abduction. The blood's another story; tethered to cracks in the car seat I found cotton fibers, matching swabs... not a hundred percent brand match, but it came from a swab."
She hung up without remembering to say goodbye; she woke Eric.
"You nailed it; the blood was smeared *with a cue tip!*"
He didn't wake up well. He rolled away.
"Lemme me be... ten more minutes."

Coffee always got him out of the sack. It percolated musically while she reviewed last night's work; gets better with each kill; how many kills did this twisted fucker have? Would there be enough clues to catch his twisted fucking ass before he attacked *again?*

Dropping bacon into the seasoned cast-iron skillet, the hissing, spattering nitrate aroma finally got her lover vertical. He lumbered in and grabbed a cup.

"What did you say 'bout blood?"

"Bill says it was planted with a cue tip. We gotta catch this perp, before he kills any more girls!"
Her eyes smoked with hatred; there was no use arguing with her.
"OK, I'm with you, but the boss won't authorize me... OR you, so we'll do this on our own time 'til we get something... COOL?"

"COOL!"

She put down the coffee and hugged his rugged ass; he looked so good in boxers.

GATHERING

Late that evening, they got together. Dunn, Blacklock and Sangreal; sounded like a law firm. They didn't have much, other than a LACK of evidence. So they worked with that. Dunn went first.

"Ok, we've got planted trace... We've got a dead perp named Sandoval, who never did fit Eric's profile. How convenient the perp died, hah? I mean, Sandoval's not here to dispute it, right?"
Eric corrected him.
"Actually, Sandoval's death *MIGHT NOT* play to his hand. He hoped Sandoval would go down for it, but now the *real perp* has more risk of exposure."
Sarah cut to the chase.
"*FUCK* the unsub's worries. Let's nail his ass! What can we do? *What do we KNOW?*"

The apprentice profiler scribbled on a legal pad.
"First, he is intelligent and organized. Two; this is NOT his first rodeo. Three, good computer skills. Four;..."
Dunn the plodder interrupted.
"How can you say that?"
Eric downshifted.
"There were no other prints on Sandoval's car... no friends. Ergo, the perp *was a stranger.*"
The other two were silent, failing to see his point.
"Ergo, he HAD TO PICK Sandoval from *somewhere.* Our man probably targeted Sandoval the old-fashioned way; the Internet. To me, that spells 'good with computers'..."
Sarah spurred him.
"Ok, so he's good with computers. *Next item!*"

"Four; affinity for young girls, ten to twelve maybe, but prepubescent, definitely. Five; obsessed with blonds."

He saw Dunn's frown as need for buttressing.
"The hair strands at the scene; shoulder length, and his victims will have blue eyes; we're looking for a highly intelligent, organized, baby-wasp-killer."

Before Dunn trained in forensics, he minored in biology in Montana. Until then, he never thought his hunting skills might be useful in forensics.
"When I hunt an animal, I want to know where it eats, drinks and hides."
Sarah took the cue.
"He *eats* little blond-haired, blue-eyed girls.*"
"Do I go where there's one elk or a *big herd?*"
Eric chimed in.
"Pageants, girl scouts, swimming pools, fund-raiser car washes, acting schools... Got any others, guys?"
Eric nailed it; they couldn't think of others.

Dunn popped a beer.
"When I find a herd, I sit my ass down where they can't see or smell me, I take my time, size up a real trophy."
The profiler also grabbed a beer.
"That would play to his organized methods..."
Sarah's eyes smoked with hatred.
"And to his sick version of foreplay; *He gets off on it...* sitting there in the middle of the herd."
They didn't realize how closely they had profiled Eastbrook, with just a bit of thinking outside the box.

"The casebooks are full of killers that loved to be right under the precinct window, eavesdropping. Kemper loved to hang out in a cop bar, hearing them discuss the murders he'd just committed. I'm puttin' it down... Six; hangs out where cops and young GIRLS congregate. Seven; good social skills; blends in with society.

Eric was on a roll; without his boss breathing down his neck, he was free to extrapolate.

"Eight; he's between 40 and 60"

It was Sarah's turn to challenge.

"How can you *possibly* know his age?"

He drained the beer before answering.

"Impulsive young men leave clues. A week's pay says this guy's over fifty."

"Nine; SMOOTH TALKER. You can't eat lamb if you scare the ewe. Mothers see him as the safest man in a room. They'd probably let him drive their daughters home. NOT that he would, but his sheep's clothing *IS* that good. I'll bet this guy holds power; PTA, preacher, teacher, *something.* I'm listing it."

So there it was; they had their ten commandments for finding a perverted unsub sonofabitch.

"OK, if we're gonna catch this asshole, we need to do like Bill said; hunt him like a gun-shy, sagacious fuckin' animal. I think we can catch him."

For Dunn, it was a big leap; his training was in the scientific method. Now Sangreal was asking the lab rat to bungee jump in the dark, without even checking the cord. It was scary, but intoxicating. Sarah was ready. When it came to stalking pedophiles, she'd do anything, to fill the hole in her soul.

"Ok, let's get started! We'll cross check PTA lists, girls' groups, talent agencies, get a warrant to search the…"

"Whoa, Sara, *WHOAH*… we don't have cause and we sure as all hell don't have official sanction."

Eric nodded.

"He's right, Honey. Right now we're as invisible as our target; we're just three normal civilians, doin' a little freelancing."

Sarah slowed, impatient but tempered.

"Ok; citizens, just checkin' the scene; got it… *I got it.*"

Before they broke up, Dunn posed one last question.
"Ya know, there's one thing I don't get... HOW does this guy manage to abduct his prey? These are ten year-olds, right? They've seen school films. They've got friends around 'em, and their parents warnin' about strangers, so... *how the hell does he nab 'em?*"

Eric shrugged casually.
"Remember when you were ten; you'd climb high in a tree, without a care about hospitals or bone grafts. Your mom says; *"Don't climb so high"*. Hell, even if you *listened,* it sounded more like a challenge than reprimand. Now imagine someone on the ground, a facilitator, urging you to climb higher; *you'd hear THAT*, wouldn't you? Well, she heard the words she wants to hear. He's the charmer, she's the snake."

"Pied Piper" interjected Sarah.
"Playing a tune and the rats follow; no noise, commotion... Oh, I can't wait to catch this prick. When they stick a needle in his vein, I'm gonna be there!"

STANDSTILL

In spite of the Amber Alerts, grassroot support, fliers and TV spots, Tiffany Simpson's story gradually morphed into last-page news. The billboards had new cases, the press had fresh sob stories. Jennifer heard it in the cop's voice, too; they were still *'doing everything we can',* but it didn't sound like so much, any more.

Her child was a minnow gulped by a shark. Or even if she hadn't been gulped, even if she'd had just a near-miss, the wake turbulence put her in a tailspin, flailed her scales and obliterated her reference point; she'd never find her way home.

The candlelight vigils ceased; handmade banners proclaiming undying love and remembrance became tattered and dew-stained. Tiffany's case was in no-man's land; gone too long for Tempera banners, but not long enough for a milk carton mugshot. Her peers thought of other things. Shelly was the wildebeest, shredded by lions while the herd went back to grazing; an acceptable, regrettable loss. The herd knew the reality; yes, there were lions, but they're feeding now... Next page, please.

On the eighteenth day, Jennifer finally caved to the grim reality; her kid wasn't coming home. She vowed to toughen up and move on. It wouldn't be easy, but it had to be done.

She called the local mortuary for a referral to a decent church; it was time to have a ceremony. She thought back to when she used to go to church; it felt weird. But when she hung up the phone and it immediately rang, mother's instinct gripped her... Only death rings so heavy.

"Hello?"

"Jennifer?"

"Yes..."

With no tactful way to bash her world, she went for it.

"Officer Miller; sorry to upset you. We located a body and need to rule out your child as the victim."

The handset got heavier; the cop wouldn't be calling without good reason.

"Are you sure? I mean, do you think it's MY SHELLY?"

"We DON'T KNOW yet, but time of death coincides. We're sending DNA and records, to find out. We'll get back to you as soon as we know. I can't imagine how you must feel... I'm sorry."

There was no answer; Jennifer fainted. A few minutes later, she woke up and re-dialed Miller.

"Officer, I'm sorry. I sort of... fainted."

Miller choked back her tears and tried to sound firm. A cop should always sound firm.

"OH... understandable. We'll let you know EITHER WAY, as soon as we know. Goodbye, Mrs. Simpson."

Jennifer hung up and reached for the booze.

COMPULSORIES

The last pageant of the season would be in Austin. David was to be an alternate. It was something of an honor, because fifty-odd candidates nationwide who ranked under him, would kill to be an alternate.

It would only take a typical traveler two days, but he would burn five, so he could brag about being a judge at every coffee shop and bistro; it netted girls before.

It was almost two full months since his last orbit, with... what was it... Simmons... Simon, something like that. At first it was easy to relive the stealing, squealing, squirming, bleeding... the terror in those eyes turned his dick to granite.

But memories fade. He tried to refresh them by sniffing her panties, but the scent faded, too. This left him with earrings, the only trophy he kept of Simpson; yeah, that was it, *Shelly Simpson*. But the tiny turquoise posts couldn't do it for him, although they HAD matched her eyes oh, so well.

He was left with masturbating to videos of past victims. But even videotapes lose their impact with too much repetition. He faced the obvious; it was time for another orbit. He knew enough of his illness to recognize... and embrace it.

The third night on the road brought him to a Roastwell, New Mexico motel. Donning a disguise, he registered and soon found the same room he'd seen before; twin beds, swiveling TV, cabled down remote, clean bathroom, bible and flimsy ice pail.

Then he drove to a shopping mall. He parked away from those pesky spy cameras. The disguise was simple; blond wig, zero-mag horn-rimmed glasses, saltwater fishing cap, jeans, jogging shoes, Led Zeppelin tee shirt. Not that his young victims would know the band; nobody sees fifty-year-olds. They can get away with anything.

Entering the huge double doors, the onrushing olfactory tsunami blasted him; buttered popcorn, fast food grease, perfumes and hair gels topped the crest. Birds flew above the landscaped centerpiece. Echoing voices gave it a cathedral-like hum.

Arcades usually held a berth somewhere near center, usually down a side alley. Parents could shop, while psychologically near their quarter-gobbling youngsters. He ambled, using his 'ignore me' shuffle.

Three shops from the arcade, he bought a small bag of malt balls. When he entered the arcade, he put a twenty in the change machine. A light came on. The machine buzzed, then puked out eighty coins, some cold, others hot; it was a busy joint.

The synthetic cave held many young boys. Their lack of hygiene, budding sexuality and pheromones reeking, the stench fairly nauseated the pedophile. He found three machines that catered to girls; an old Ms. Pac Man and two pinball games colored in lavender, pink and chartreuse.

He went out and sat on a bench, nibbling candy and biding time. The adjacent theater marquis said it would soon release girls from some bullshit anime unicorn movie. Eastbrook targeted PG movies, since they entranced young girls, lowering whatever suspicion they might have.

Soon streams of young kids exited; predictably, most were girls. He hurried into the arcade ahead of the prospective mark. He chose a game near the Lady Pac Man; a golf game, not that it mattered. As long as it looked like an old dude might play it, that was enough. Two games later, he had surveyed twelve girls; only one blonde, but she had busts, which meant hair down there. Deciding to call it a night, he stood up. Then his mark walked in; she was perfect.

She came in with her big brother. Eastbrook knew the deal; the teen's trip was conditional upon taking Sissy; girls that age loved to tattle, so Mom's little spy would keep Junior honest.

Junior gave her some quarters, then disappeared into the writhing maggot mass of boys swarming over the hottest game. His little sister could catch fire and he wouldn't notice. Sissy sauntered straight for the Lady Pac Man, the oldest game in the haunt.

He started his pre-launch checklist. He spied just one camera above the mass of youngsters, pointed at the cash register. He checked for security guards. Then he remembered the fliers he'd seen; it was a pro rodeo weekend. That would explain the scanty security; the whole adult population was out watching a bunch of redneck assholes getting bucked off bulls. He double-checked on Junior; the kid was vying for playing position. It was as good as it got.

Eastbrook rolled several quarters to the mark. The sharp-eyed Barbie saw the metallic flash, bent down, picked them up; he got a beaver shot... pink panties. He started drooling. She was perfect. Her angelic face, the epitome of innocence, set his guts into a swirling tornado of lust and desire and hatred. He put on the baby-conning smile to conceal it. As usual, it worked like a charm.

"Sir, did YOU drop these?"

"Oh, yes, thank you… you're very honest. Why don't you keep two, for being honest… and brave. Most girls are scared to talk to strangers, *but… you're brave!*"

Melissa swelled with pride. She spotted the candy.

"Yeah, they tell us at school, allatime… never talk to strangers… 'specially *Niggers*."
Eastwood smiled; it would be tough pickings for a black pedophile in this redneck town. He opened his palm to show a handful of quarters.
"Here, take more… I've got plenty."

She reached into the outstretched palm, snagged two coins, accidentally touching his palm; cool and moist, like he was shy. She was too young to recognize it as nervous anticipation. She played the quarters. He reached out with more coins and smiled, the viper's eyes cold with evil. Luckily, she stared at the coins. He used his chalky, child stealing voice.

"My name's Bobby; what's yours?"
"Melissa Brooks; I'm ten!"
"Melissa, that's a nice name. Do you like dogs?"
He showed a picture of a fox terrier puppy with white fur and black spots.
"This is Bernie, my puppy. I have to go pet him or he gets lonely. I'll come back with more quarters."
He got up to go, relying upon her natural innocence… he was rewarded, as usual.
"Can I pet Bernie, too?"
Time to set the hook.
"Oh, I don't know… he's shy; would you be *NICE?*"
She was already nodding.
"I'm nice to puppies…"
"OK, if you *PROMISE* not to scare Bernie."

Smiling happily, the girl was dead already; she just didn't know it yet. Eastbrook walked out, Melissa in tow. She couldn't wait to pet that little dog.

He looked like just another dad leading his kid home. Just as they got to the RV, he held out his hand.
"Here; hold these quarters while I open the door. OK, watch out Bernie doesn't lick you too much!"
She leaped into the RV, calling for the imaginary pup.
"Here, Bernie…"
She was confused when the mask sealed her mouth. But being a smart girl, before the gas knocked her out, she got it; she was too brave for her own good.

He taped her, tossed her on the bed and fired up the RV. He booted the GPS system. Since it was Friday night in a redneck town, he'd have to avoid the local make-out spots and the best poaching roads.
Ah, but THAT was the rub; he didn't know the area. As he drove toward the desert, the adrenaline rush cleared. In its place came the dread of not having a plan; the urge forced him into unfamiliar terrain, quite literally.

It would be folly to venture into remote areas; his rig would stick out like a hooker in church. His headlights would attract any game wardens looking for poachers or deputies hunting teens screwing in the desert. Then he thought of Border Patrol… He cursed his lack of control, which was getting worse lately.

All he could think of was getting in the bedroom with the tattletale bitch. He had to suck the drool down to keep from dribbling on the steering wheel. He thought of taking her to his motel room, but that was foolhardy. Just then, he spotted a sign; *"Rest stop, 15 miles"* Where better for an RV to blend?

When the rest stop came into view, it was perfect for his needs; a small cinder-block shit-house, one door for skirts, one for slacks. A sign indicated hot showers and tourist information, both closed at sundown. He parked far from the single floodlight. His monitor showed a fifty-yard sphere of darkness. Save for the floodlit pathway to the shitters, it was dark as hell.

He hoped he hadn't given her too much nitrous... not like that first kill, so long ago. That was a real drag; he accidentally killed his fun. But this time he'd pulled the gas much sooner... she'd be coming out of it soon. If not, he'd have to start anyway; it wasn't as much fun, but time was scarce; she'd be reported missing soon.

He reached into the top drawer for a plastic sheet with several beauty marks. One looked perfect for her. He placed it under the girl's right infraorbital foramen, halfway to the corner of her mouth, where his tattle-tail bitch cousin had one.

A few strokes of lipstick got her lips like Peggy's. Just then, the monitor showed movement; several people walked to and from the bathrooms... He got off on it, having people go by, within mere yards, totally oblivious. He would use this variation in future orbits.

It wasn't long before she was bleeding, pleading, writhing and heaving. She was dead and of no more use by eleven; a quickie, of sorts, for the predator that normally took his time. When he finished showering, his thoughts turned to re-entry; he got scared.

He was in strange country. There was no time to freeze her, either, because he had to go to Austin. He didn't want a body in his freezer, with his rig in the parking lot for the week-long show.

Time to improvise... He hit the highway. A sign said *'Next rest stop 60 Miles'*. Hopefully he could find a place to dump the body, then get a good night's rest. He wanted to look good for that pageant.

He drove along, reviewing his checklist. First, he left no DNA. The only penetrating he'd done was with his tools. All the semen and hair and prints were only on his tools and her panties, which would stay with him. Fifteen miles later he saw a sign indicating an exit. Slowing the rig down fast, he barely got it stopped before he ran out of pavement.

The underpass was just for a seldom-used trail, so some rancher could drive his cattle from one pathetic desert cactus patch to the other on the far side of the highway. At each pasture were barbed wire gates blocking cows and unauthorized human passage.

It might be weeks before anybody used this underpass. Seeing no headlights for miles, he scurried to get the body into the tumbleweed; it took longer to get the rig back up to highway speed.

To the uncaring night clerk, Eastbrook looked like just another asshole tourist, coming back after last call. That he checked out at six was all the same to the clerk; most tourists were eager to get the fuck out of Roastwell, off to wherever they were headed. If you've seen one Saguaro, you've seen 'em all.

The clerk hated the desert. He wanted to move to Southern California; Gander City, maybe… wherever there was some action.

CONCENTRATION

After one week of after-hours effort, the trio met for a briefing, this time at Eric's place. Sarah was frustrated.

"Well, I checked out everybody with influence over her; all clean. I don't have *ANY suspects*! now what?"

Eric knew, but there was no sense pissing off his girlfriend by being a know-it-all. Things had been strained enough between them, lately. He waited for Dunn to correct her thinking... Sure enough, he coughed it up, right on cue.

"Well, Sarah, you slipped back into your cop's training. Remember when Eric said this guy's invisible?"

Her look said she drew a blank.

"We're cops, trained to catch morons that have a rap sheet, but... *this guy i*s another species. So when you say you have *NO* suspects, I say you've got plenty of SUSPECTS... *got it?"*

She got it. She just didn't like men trying to boss her around, but she concealed it. After all, Dunn had the same goal, catching perverts. Eric had seen the look before. He picked up the torch.

"Yep, it's like a guy driving SLOWER than the limit; he's *suspicious!"*

Dunn trussed the concept.

"Our guy's a ghost. People hold him in high regard. Nobody sees the wizard behind the curtain."

Sarah was pissed off, but she nodded.

"OK, OK, I got it. I'm looking for Mr. Squeaky Fuckin' Clean, pedophile rapist-child-killer, whose-neighbors-love-him-enough-to-defend him… *I got it.*"
Both men watched her brown eyes smolder; until they quit smoking, it was pointless to speak at all.

Bill uncorked the wine, to pour over the silence.
Half a glass later, he spoke softly, an ally of unlimited patience.

"I have to tell you guys; it feels like we're hunting this asshole the wrong way. We've questioned potential witnesses, but our unsub's invisible, so of course they don't have leads for us; it's time to reformat."

He savored his Cabernet before continuing.
"One time I hunted a Stone ram up in the Wrangells. He'd bed on north-facing slopes while the herd bedded on south slopes, where the grass grew better. I tried hunting the herd, hoping he'd come to them. Then I started scaling those ice-covered northerns and sure enough; three days later I bagged him while he headed for his afternoon bed… Anyhow, he targets blonde girls and he's squeaky clean. For a minute, let's work with just those facts… Where is our 'ram' MOST LIKELY to hang?"
Eric nodded; "Where there are lots of blonde girls."

Sarah's sarcasm pierced the dialogue; they'd already covered this, and useless repetition made her impatient.
"True"
Dunn pointed a finger upward;
"Now, *which places* hold high concentration?"
Eric opened the salvo.
"Beaches, cheerleading, dance studios, modeling agencies, pageants, wet tee shirt contests… right? I can narrow it down *a whole shitload, right now.*"

He reached in his bag for the studio shots of Michelle.

Dunn's eyes plodded for details. Sarah went straight to the point.

"No wonder she got abducted! *She was TROLLING for pedophiles!* She sexualized her, campaigned her! Then he targets her... learns where she lives, when she's alone. He stalks her and catches her when her mom's at work. Then Uncle Phil..."
It was the first time she uttered his name out loud. She tried to cover.
"Or Bill or John does whatever he wants with... *her.*"

The men pretended not to notice.
"Lookit; lip gloss, makeup, frills, shakes booty like a Vegas stripper. Christ! The only thing missing is the stripper's pole! She promenades her kid, never caring that someone in the audience or panel might be a filthy stinking... pervert."

Dunn interrupted, in agreement.
"Jeezus, when you put it like that, it's more like pornography, with parents as enablers."
She nodded before he finished.
"The definition of obscene... if it gets you erect, it's porn. Well, to the audience, it's an innocent batch of little girls. But to a pedophile it's... a whack-off buffet."

Eric chimed in;
"I spoke with Janine Wilson, a pageant organizer. Ten bucks gets you in the stands. Another twenty gets you backstage; for less than the cost of a lousy lap dance, a pedophile can be arm's length from his prospects."
Dunn countered.
"Maybe so, but most of the audience is parents or people scouting competition; if there *were* pedophiles, they'd be hard to spot."

The rest of the wine went into the goblets and they drank in silence; it was a damned good Redwood Valley Pinot Noir.

Finally Sarah queried.
"So… he's invisible, sits in the stands, gets hard watching Barbies dance strut? *That's* who we're hunting? *Fuck me…*"

Eric's mind floated in that three-glasses-of-good-wine state, between warmth and the urge to get really stinking drunk, fuck, then puke it all up later. Then something jogged his memory.

"Sarah… what did you say?"
"This guy sits in the stands, gets har…"
"*NO*, earlier… You said; *'someone in the audience or panel might be a… pedophile'…* right?"

She shrugged impatiently; he could be so persnickety.
"Right… *SO WHAT?*"
"So, what did you mean by *'panel?'*"
Now it was the plodding Dunn to add to the equation;
"Judging… she meant *JUDGING PANEL…*"

The power of her words struck home. Eric interjected.
"WOW I know I said it, but… *a judge?*"

Sarah helped the profile take form.
"Well, what better sheep's' clothing? Just think of the psychological leverage… *it's unbelievable!*"

Dunn reigned in his eager partner;
"Easy girl… whoa… let's not get ahead of ourselves; it's just a theory. We'll start tomorrow. Meanwhile, why don't we uncork *this?*"

He lifted a bottle of Navarro Zinfandel; the real grunt work would start in the morning, but for now, the fruity coastal varietal demanded center stage. Either that or they were too numb for further shop talk.

EPIPHANY

Darwin sat across from Kaylee Parker. He longed for this date ever since he'd met her at her first dog-handling seminar. It took two years to work up the guts to ask. He wasn't much on rejection, but he'd seen her with guys who looked like real losers, so he finally asked her out, when he returned Beau and Duke after the Simpson search. He praised the dogs and popped the question; would she sometime, maybe if she weren't too busy to go out with a loser like him, like to have dinner?

To which the freewheeling bombshell said; *"Why not?"* He set a date for three weeks, to give her plenty of time to back out. She didn't.

They waited for Cokes and burgers, her image of haut cuisine. With the usual first-date awkwardness, they tried to think of common ground for conversation. All she could think of was why didn't he take her out earlier. Meanwhile, all he could think of was dogs.

"So, how's the seminars coming, Kay?"

She toyed with her straw."Oh, OK; I'm just starting to get known, ya know?"

The convo dead-ended. He tried to jump start it.

"Boy, it sure was nice to work with *YOUR* hounds... Thanks again for loaning them to me?"

Her dogs warmed her heart; "Sure. You can use 'em any time. I'm still surprised they didn't scent *anything.*

It must've been a cold trail."

Then the dumb bastard fumbled the ball.

"Oh, well... they did wail once, while we were walking down the street, but their noses weren't down?"

Kaylee straightened up, looking straight in his eyes.
"They WAILED?"

It was more accusation than question.
"MY hounds NEVER WAIL! That was red-hot scent!"
He shrank in the booth.
"OH? I thought it was just a bitch in heat somewhere, 'cuz it was just a momentary whiff, and then both dogs went quiet again?"

She frowned.
"Well, maybe so; I wasn't there, so I can't say, but it sounds weird. Did you hear any other vocalizations?"

The waiter brought food and left before he answered.
"Not really... they were gosh-darned quiet, all day, except for one little whoof Beau made earlier... just a little whoof."

Kaylee lost her interest in burgers and dates; her laser-green eyes bored right through him...

"WHAT?"
"WHERE WERE YOU WHEN HE *WHOOFED?"*

Her words weren't meant for her date, but her slowest student, the stupid prick that missed Beau's only point. She worked hard to get that signal... not loud enough to alert nearby perps, but just enough for the handler to hear. And this dumb bastard missed it. His stock just went down; Black Fucking Monday sort of down.

Feeling his chances slipping, Townsend stammered.
"Me? I was, lemme see... I was standing on Pastor...

I mean... Dave Eastbrook's lawn? He's really nice; he goes to my church? He used to be my deacon, but now he's retired; he's a..."
"Fuck Eastbrook! Where was Beau?"
Townsend always rambled when nervous.
"He was, uh... I'm not really sure? I was talking to Deaco... I mean Pastor... Dave... we were, uh, next to his RV? Beau was sniffin' the drainpipe, I think? Dave cleaned some... he said Beau sniffed fish guts?"

Kaylee could barely avoid bitch-slapping the dolt... The thought of a bad guy escaping drove her crazy. She tried to be tactful.
"YOU FUCKIN' *IDIOT*"
So much for tact.
"How many times did we go over this? Each dog has its point... Beau and Duke give a quiet little whoof... *THAT'S HOW I FUCKIN' TRAINED 'EM!"*

His vacant look proved it; the dumb bastard forgot.

"DON'T YOU FUCKIN' *REMEMBER?"*

The churchgoer recoiled at the sudden Satanic shift; he could never marry a woman that used profanity. Still, she had a point; he dimly recalled the lesson; a warm May afternoon. Her full bosom and wafting perfume dulled his already dull wit. Most of that lesson was wasted on trying not to get a hard-on in front of everybody.

"Darwin, you blew it! My dogs coulda wrote; 'pedophile' in the sand! Beau was pointing scent!"
She got up and started walking out of the restaurant.
"Where are you going, Kaylee?"
Over her shoulder she yelled her contempt.
"DATE'S OVER, MORON... gotta call the cops."

Under her breath she muttered...
"How could I date such a loser?"

LUST

Kaylee's first call fell on deaf ears; they already had a suspect, the late Crystobal Sandoval, with the vic's DNA in his car. So there wasn't any point getting lathered up about some dog whoofing at an RV a month ago, especially one belonging to Dave Eastbrook, one of law enforcement's biggest supporters, fine civilian with a squeaky-clean record.

Kaylee hung up, exasperated at the arrogant prick's knee-jerk dismissal. It pissed her off to have such a hot lead dying in such stupid ears. Then she thought of the hunk she'd seen at crime scenes and her seminars.

His cell phone vibrated on the counter; an electronic rattlesnake, buzzing with lethal news. He looked at his teammates and opened it.
"Sangreal."
She wasted no time with pleasantries; they'd come later, maybe.
"Eric? Kaylee Parker... from the *dog seminars?*"

He knew that low, throaty voice; a mental picture formed. Full blouse, hazel-green eyes, lusty bedroom look. Too bad he was already tight with Blacklock or...
"You know, the *K-9 classes?*"
"Oh, sure I remember; what can I do ya for, Kaylee?"

Sarah knew it; that bitch was after Eric. She'd seen her giggling and wiggling it for Eric at a dog seminar. Whatever her oh, so important message might be, the undertone was SEX in the tall grass, pure and simple. It pissed her off; ust when she was learning to trust a man, this slutty bitch was trying to steal him.

But Eric didn't look guilty; he looked curious. He turned the speakerphone on, thinking it would be better if all three crime fighters heard it together; especially Sarah. He knew how she got, with the first whiff of jealousy.

"You're on speaker phone, Kaylee. Go ahead."

Her honey-thick voice poured over the airways. Dunn, pre-horned from the wine, started getting a hard-on.

"I have news regarding the Simpson case, but they won't listen to me at headquarters; I figured you might be more receptive."

"Sure; what is it?"

She wouldn't make the same mistake she made with headquarters; thinking they blew her off because she didn't provide enough information, she'd give him the whole story.

"I know it's late in the case, and whatever evidence might already be destroyed, but *i just found out...* I let Townsend work my hounds that day; I had the flu. Anyhow, Beau pointed but the dumb ass ignored it."

"*OH yeah?* Where and when?"

"The day they searched Sandoval's place. Apparently, Townsend's a good buddy with the guy, Eastbrook; lives off Sepulveda, on Connestoga. He said my dog whoofed when he sniffed his RV... Eric, my bloodhounds only point when they're certain. I'd stake my reputation on it. Tiffany Simpson either touched it, leaned against it or went inside. I wasn't there, so I don't know the scenting conditions, but IF Beau whoofed, he had the vic's scent. That's why I called you. If you need me for anything, call me. Bye Bye."

The trio looked at each other, nonplussed.

Sarah loathed the bitch for her choice of words; 'trust me', 'reputation' and *'need me FOR ANYTHING..."*

Dunn was thinking about a search warrant. Sangreal was trying to get Kaylee's scent out of his head. It took a moment to get his mind back on task.
"I think our search just got A *WHOLE LOT EASIER!* Let's check this dude out; what do ya say?"

Bill headed straight home to his laptop. Eric headed for the station. Sarah stayed right there in the apartment. Booting the computer, her heart wasn't in her work; the bitch was trying to steal her man. She wondered if he *really was* going to his office; *'if you need me for anything'...* covered a lot of ground.

She went online to search Eastbrook. In mere minutes she had his blog; recently sold his stores, rich, degree in computer science. He was an ex pastor, had links to non-denominational churches wherever his stores were. The pictures slowly filled in from top to bottom; Sarah made a note to defrag her computer.

There were shots with congregations, his stores, with staff posed around the man... and always, that same forged smile. Some thumbnails showed him donating; orphanages, burn wards and of course, law enforcement. To Sarah, it looked like a politician's campaign; the broadest base of appeal with no demographic overlap. None of the photos showed him with family.

One thumbnail caught her eye; He and two other adults held clipboards, judging Barbies; a Freudian slip. After a whole page of self-aggrandizing shots, this one practically said; *"By the way, I look at little girls; here are my credentials."*

She opened that thumbnail; pageant tips... potential starlets should go here, there... giving the site an air of authenticity. She clicked on the do's and don'ts.

A beautiful Asian girl, probably nine or ten; her only sin was a visible bit of panties; *"Contestant eliminated in preliminary; WINNERS observe every detail."*

She clicked the box to its right; gorgeous Hispanic, thin frame, light enough to pass for Caucasian, long hair, lashes, big smile... but the kid wasn't going anywhere; *"Baton ends not symmetrical."*

She got the gist of it; don'ts were African-American, Mexican-American, Asian; the biggest don't; "If you're not a wasp, we'll swat you."

She clicked on a "Do"; blonde-haired, blue-eyed Barbie filled in; *"Costume flawless. DO ensure yours is, too."*
The next one showed another Cauckie with a flute. *"Do be sure to have a viable skill."*

Each subsequent shot showed a cookie-cutter Barbie. The more she looked, the hotter grew her hatred. Dialing Eric's cell, she got him while he was inside his truck. He slid the phone open while driving.
"Hi, honey... what's up?"
"You're in your *truck?* I thought you were at the precinct?"

"Oh yeah, I WAS goin' there, but then that Kaylee girl called me. She wants to take the dogs by Eastbrook's."

Her anger transferred to that slutty cunt trying to take her man. Eric never referred to any woman as '*that* anybody' before... It held danger.

"You're gonna SEE HER *NOW?* Eric, it's MIDNIGHT!"

She instantly regretted her words, better spoken by a clingy insecure housewife trying to keep her hubby from the clutches of some stripper-hussy lapdance-blowjobbing homewrecker. Eric didn't miss it, either.

"OH; well, come over if you want, but hurry; she says his RV's parked there right now."

Sarah hated the trap; if she went, she'd be the insecure bitch trying to control Eric, too weak to know his mind in the presence of a hottie. But if she didn't go, those tits would be wiggling for her man. It pissed her off, to think how fast and far they were drifting… from catching the pervert, of course. She could only give him some rope, then see if he'd hang himself.
After all, how much did she really know about him? They'd only been living together three months. Maybe he was just like all the rest of 'em; let 'em sniff a woman and they go from zero to full-rutting pig in three seconds. She killed the pregnant silence.

"No, you guys go check it out. Call me later. Bye."

She snapped the razor phone shut, sick of men. She reached for the vodka. Two drinks later, the green-eyed monster arose. She could see Eric riding that bitch in the back of his pickup bed, fake nails digging into his tight, muscular ass… high heels gouging into his hamstrings, greedy with lust, the husky voice moaning, while Eric pounded himself deeper into her, over and over.

Struggling to erase the vision, she drank more vodka and transplanted Eastbrook's image over her jealousy. But the pervert's image faded fast; her twisted stepfather suddenly blotted out everything.

His reeking stench filled her nostrils; she felt him coming inside her, pawing her breasts with his left hand, throttling her with his right, forcing her head back over the bathtub edge until it felt like her neck would snap. Struggling to breathe, frightened and unable to get away, the thirteen-year-old could only sob and squirm; and the sick bastard enjoyed that more. His raspy voice rang in her ears when he finally stopped ejaculating; *"You tell anyone, I'll kill you. I'll kill your fuckin' mother, too… just for the fun of it."* He raped her often, until she got the chance to run.

Sarah tried to tell her mother, but it failed; twice divorced and losing what was left of her looks, Winifred clung to the last meal ticket she'd be likely to snag. If she lost *him,* Winnie would be on her own, waiting tables in cheap dives. Besides, her daughter would soon grow up and leave, and a woman just had to watch out for herself, didn't she?

Phil Dean was a house painter; made good money, eager to spend it on her and Sarah. So she Spackled over the cracks in his character flaws, then painted over them with a double coating of denial... the paint was barely dry. She dismissed the accusations as mere fantasies of a jealous, love-starved thirteen year-old girl-woman.

Come to think of it, Sarah *WAS* developing awfully fast. Hormone-crazed girls concocted all sorts of fantasies. Denial, ah, sweet denial, the patron saint of the pervert; rears its head in thousands of homes every night. And, predatory men like Phil were always quick to exploit it.

Sarah came away from it in fairly good style. She became an emancipated minor, found a job in a law firm. The senior partner took a liking to her. He gave her a key to his private office, where she slept, showered and primped, but at school before the lawyers arrived. Graduated with honors, too, without inviting her mother to the ceremony.

She quickly rose from janitor to filing clerk to paralegal. But over time, she saw too many crooks get off; she wanted to be a cop or a prosecutor, to keep those child-raping assholes from hurting more people. Then one night after the others left, one slimy lawyer put the moves on her. Her next stop was the academy. She never looked back. Forensics became her goal.

The ringing phone snapped her out of her ten-thousandth Uncle Phil flashback. She put the glass down and picked up. Eric's voice sounded creamy.

"Hi, Honey; we just got back from Eastbrook's... the dogs couldn't find scent, but they acted confused. Kaylee says..."

Sarah couldn't hear anything else... Two hours ago it was *"That Kaylee girl"* now it's *'Kaylee says this...* in a few more hours, Kaylee would be 'Honey." Hot blood rushed in her ears. She hung up; he was still talking.

She soon found herself driving, with the full moon rising, lighting her convertible in blue. Her beau was out there with that fat cunt... She drove faster... headed for Eastbrook's place. Lusty visions flooded her mind. She saw them screwing in the truck bed, legs in the moonshine, ass-crack and balls banging the cold metal truck bed.

Consumed with jealousy, she drove past Eastbrook's residence. It took two blocks before she noticed and retraced. She drove slowly, to catch 'em humping on some side street, probably.

But none of the side streets held her lover and the Kaylee whore-bitch. This didn't help her mood, though, because fear of the unknown drives more rage than any known fact ever could.

It just put them back at her place, probably in a shower; that man could fuck like a stallion in a shower. She saw soapsuds dripping off big pink nipples, her man licking them off the bitch moaning with lust, her fat ass flattened against the shower tile.

Truth be told, it wasn't such a fat ass; that was the jealousy talking. That bitch had an enviable ass. No mortal man could...

She pulled over, a half-block from Eastbrook's darkened residence. The RV was parked on the side street, under massive Sycamores whose canopy shaded out the streetlight. A few fallen leaves adorned the windshield, lightly dusted with alkali; the bastard had been in the desert, probably raping and burying girls. Men were such pigs.

Somebody up the street left sprinklers on. Water flowed by the RV in a wide, shallow stream. She couldn't find a single wet paw print... if that bitch went there with her hounds, the water would've attracted them. Someone was lying; probably her sex-pig-asshole, soon-to-be-ex lover.

She went to the shadows under the Sycamores to look for tracks, but she didn't have her flashlight to confirm it. She went back for it, getting angrier at each stride. Asshole Eric was banging "that Kaylee tramp"... She *could feel it.*

Sarah found her flashlight. The beam illuminated her forensic tools; the lock picks caught her eye. In the nether-world, noir-genius of the drunk, a rash plan hatched. She would one-up that Kaylee slut *AND* her fucking dogs.

She staggered back to the RV with her crime scene case. The cheap lock was no match for a woman scorned. The Winnemako was squeaky clean, just like the cocksucker that owned it. She taped the bed covers and carpets for hair strands. Then she raped the bathroom J-trap, using a crochet hook. In just two minutes, Sara found herself outside the re-locked RV. If that child-raping asshole was guilty, she'd know it soon enough. Staggering back to her car, she felt pretty fucking good.

The surprising adrenaline rush of the B&E fueled her excitement; now she knew why burglars did it. Hell, it even made her forget about Eric for a while. Stopping off at a convenience store, she picked up more vodka; a woman can never have too much vodka. Guzzling while driving, Sara made it home without crashing or getting busted. Or so she thought. She awoke not at home, but in her best friend's flat. Libby Sheridan was opening the front door.

"Hey, girlfriend, *what are YOU DOING HERE?* You have a fight with that honey of a hunk?"
Libby knew a man-hunk when she saw one, and Eric definitely qualified. Her friend rolled over and groaned. Obviously Sarah was hung over again. She went to fix a Bloody Mary, the only cure for this ailment. She sliced celery, poured vodka over shaved ice, added tomato juice, Tabasco, Worcester and fresh Wasabi, ground peppercorns and organic San Bernadino olives. If that wouldn't jump start her dear friend, nothing would.

It smelled so good, she made one for herself, too. It had been a rough night at the sawmill. May as well commiserate. She loved Sarah; hell, if she were gay, she would have married her years ago.

"OK, stop me if I'm wrong. You had wine with your forensics dudes, to discuss your secret project. I'm guessing... somewhere around the third bottle, the party broke up... How am I doin' so far?

Silence spurred her on.

"OK, then Sarah switches to the hard stuff. Since Mercury's in retrograde and there's a full moon, you got MAJORLY pissed at your honey. You drove to some ridiculous straight bar, flaunted it, probably started a fight, drove here, then passed out. Sound about right, babe?"

Sarah had heard the same speech before. There wasn't any point in refuting it, because Libby was probably right. Then she remembered; this was her day off. She guzzled the Bloody Mary... Maybe it would jog her memory.

Halfway through her second drink, the fog lifted like a roll up door in an industrial shop. The onrushing light of truth shocked her to awareness. Come to think of it, *she did have a fight*, but Eric didn't know it. The hung-over crime fighter stumbled to her car for her cell phone; but it had a dead battery.

She opened the glove box for the charger. Out came an empty vodka bottle and two baggies full of trace evidence. She recoiled in horror when she recalled the B & E. She struggled for excuses.

Well, her man *had been out with a slutty whore...* How many men can resist? If that bitch wanted him, the horny bastard was toast. Without so much as another word to Libby, she fired up the car and drove straight to the lab.

COLLUSION

Sarah entered the back door and asked Jimmy Walker to process the evidence under the table. She didn't plan to use it in an official capacity. And, since Eric was the first man she'd trusted, it held more emotional valence than it normally would have. It didn't help that Kaylee Parker bore a striking resemblance to Sara's mother, back when she was young and gorgeous enough to compete for her boyfriends. It was too twisted to think about.

She forced herself to focus on her plan; once Sarah had the shit on Eastbrook, Eric would forget all about Kaylee. Then, with three young law-minds back on track, they could get a warrant and dildo-fuck that child-raping bastard to a slow, painful death.

She went to her cubicle, even though it was her day off and she reeked of booze. Checking her voicemail, there were two messages; the usual bullshit from a man who was probably cheating.

"Hi, Honey… I couldn't reach your cell; gimme a call if you get this before morning, ok? Click."
Then, the second.
"Hi; I'm home, you're not, so I guess I'll see you tomorrow. Love ya. Bye. Click."

The first electronic alibi came when she left the phone in her car to break into Eastbrook's rig. The second came during her vodka blackout; her battery was probably dead by then.

The messages went a long way toward her forgiving him, conditional upon no hickies, fingernail scratches or guilty looks. The strong urge to swab his dick for DNA came and left. She went home to sleep it off. Late in the day, her phone woke her up, announcing a voicemail from the lab rat, Jimmy.

"I have answers for the proficiency test. Call my cell."

'Proficiency test' was code for whenever someone in the lab needed something; a paternity test here, HIV test there... anything that the boss shouldn't know about. Labbies were a tight group.

Jimmy caught her call on the first ring. He whispered. "Jesus, Sara... That hairball you gave me? Where'dya get it, a grade school bathroom? I found strands from three different, all blonde. Mixed in were hairs and shaving epi-remnants, older male; but it was compromised with bleach and god knows what else. But I still managed to sort 'em out microscopically."

Sarah went hot with anticipation; Eastbrook was not only guilty of taking Simpson, but perhaps others, too. "OK, ok... fax it to my home pc. Remember; *it's under the table.*"

Jimmy Ray nodded silently into the phone; "Got it."

He hung up, glad to have it off his desk. Proficiency tests always made him nervous; there was no telling when one might bite a guy in the ass.

Three hours later, the trio met at Dunn's place. His house was so clean, it made Sarah nervous. The lifelong bachelor was too good of a housekeeper; she vowed not to spill any wine on that gorgeous rug. Although the wine-loving Persians who wove it would probably approve, the clean-freak wouldn't.

Sangreal was ten minutes late; it didn't take long for the lovers to get into it. Yes, he'd gone with Kaylee. No, they hadn't crossed the street or let the dogs near the water... Kaylee merely walked them downwind, across the side street. And by the way, Almost four weeks after she'd been abducted, Tiffany M. Simpson's scent still told the hounds the grisly tale.

As she listened to Eric's story, Sarah's jealousy slowly dulled, until she felt guilty for suspecting him at all. When Eric finished, Dunn took over, filling in the awkward silence.

"Well, it took some doing, but I backtracked him. Wherever he lived for the last ten years, there has been a statistical increase in abduction. Not enough to pin him to the table, but it's damned sure compelling."

Dunn's hobby was insects. To pin to the table meant the first step in dissecting. It was a good metaphor; the bastard needed pinning.

Sarah gulped her wine; there was no easy way to say it... the best way was to suck in some air and just blurt it out. Let the chips fall where they may.

"Well, I sort of... broke into his RV"

The guys didn't look too shocked; they knew how much she hated perverts.
"And... I sort of... took some trace to the lab."
Now nobody was drinking.
"And, Jimmy Ray... found hair strands, all blond, unfit for DNA... He's been stealing kids and raping them *for years!* We've gotta stop him!"
Dunn chimed in;
"No shit, stop him. But, Sarah are you sure nobody saw you?"
Shaking her head for emphasis, she answered fast.

"*Nobody* saw me. I mean, I *was a bit toasted*, but it was dark and late. Besides, I was only inside for a minute. The bigger question is; how do we get a warrant?"

The query hung the group like a cheap computer with a virus. They couldn't approach higher-ups with evidence taken during an illegal B & E by a drunken forensics expert; it would kill the evidence deader than a smoked mackerel. Neither could they go to a judge and say; *Judge, we know this asshole's a killer, due to stolen evidence; how'zabout a warrant?* Eric came up with a plausible option.

"Let's just pretend yesterday didn't happen."

That was fine with Sarah; yesterday was an alcohol-induced jealous rage, which seemed unjustified now.
It was OK with Dunn, too; all yesterdays were history.
"Let's rewind to *JUST BEFORE* we sniffed and burglarized... nobody knows except us, *right?*"
"Nobody EXCEPT Kaylee Parker."
Eric defended her.
"Oh, she's OK. I prompted her before we went. Don't worry, she's on board; Kaylee hates perverts, too."

Sarah's blood flushed hot at her rival's name; how hard and long did he *'PROMPT'* that fat, sloppy whore? Eric missed her look, but he kept at it.

"So, we re-wind the clock... Remember when Kaylee called? Townsend just told her about that *first bloodhound point?* Why can't work from there?"
Dunn the plodder capped it for them.
"Well, we can sure try... We stick together, keep our story straight, and we just might nail his ass."

They finished their wine and decided to go with that story. They knew where to shop it, too; Medaris hated pedophiles too.

COVERUP

Bright and early the next morning, the trio walked into his office. Medaris knew something was up; they NEVER entered together.
"What do *YOU THREE* want?"
Eric replied first.
"Boss, we've got a situation... needs special handling. Remember that Simpson abduction?"

Of course he fuckin' remembered it! He couldn't fuckin' forget it. The fuckin' pedophile died while Medaris questioned him, the only fuckin' black mark on his whole fuckin' career. With two years left to retirement, it jeopardized his whole fuckin' pension.
"What ABOUT it?"

Dunn backed Eric.
"Well, yesterday we got a lead. One of the handlers told us her dog pointed an RV... *Eastbrook's RV.*"
Medaris knew this too; the night desk told him earlier.
"Yeah, but... what's it been, four, five weeks? Why didn't she tell us back then?"

Sarah hated to defend her slutty rival, but she hated pedophiles worse.
"*SHE* didn't find out *until yesterday, boss*; someone else handled her hounds... Townsend, I think; wasn't familiar with her dogs, so he missed the point. Just yesterday, he told her. She called us right away."

Medaris smelled a fuckin' rat;
"Called *YOU?* Why'd she call *YOU?*"

Eric parried.

"Actually, *she called Veracruz first, but he blew her off*, so she called me; she knows me from K-9 class; figured maybe I'd take her seriously."

Their boss was a detective, through and through. This reeked of a freelance job. He got pissed off.

"Bullshit, Bill said *"US."* Now you're saying *"ME"* What the hell's goin' on? Have you guys been freelancin'? Give it to me straight or get the fuck out of here!"

Medaris hated spoon-fed narratives. He was old school; he wanted facts solid enough to convict perps. Dunn caved in.

"Let's say we were *HYPOTHETICALLY freelancing*. We like Eastbrook, boss... Sarah's got unusable trace, placing multiple girls in his RV; just don't ask how she got it. Eric & the handler pointed her scent on his RV *yesterday*. And... I've been sniffin' up his ass on the internet. This guy's bad to the core. Wherever he's lived I've found rises in unsolved abduction."

Medaris shook his head. He could see the fuckin' headlines; *"PEDOPHILE DEFENDANT FREED DUE TO MULTIPLE FUCKIN' CIVIL RIGHTS VIOLATIONS."*

His posse had him in their sights, but the foundation was illegal... he fuckin' hated it.

"SONOFAFUCKIN'BITCH... we're so fuckin' LIABLE... how are we gonna fuckin' CLEAN IT UP?"

They knew a fuckin' rhetorical when they fuckin' heard one. They waited for their boss to work through it. It took a few pregnant minutes while the down-turned face got progressively redder. Then the redness faded; he found a plan.

"WHO *ELSE* knows about... *IT?"*
Sarah loved offering up the slut.
"Kaylee Parker knows, but Eric told her that…"

Medaris swore heatedly.
"FUCK ME… A FUCKIN' *CIVILIAN*? That's just *great!*
Why not a fuckin' civil rights lawyer, while we're at it!

Dunn waited for the steam to dissipate.
"Well, technically she *might not* be civilian; she
teaches K-9 officers. That might make her an agent of
the state. I ain't a lawyer, but either way, Kaylee's
cool."
Eric chimed in.
"We can trust her. She hates pedophiles."
Medaris shook his head;
"Well, we've sure got our tit in the fuckin' ringer."

The young officers knew nothing of ancient washing
machines or their proclivity for snagging laundress'
nipples. Just another old-school metaphor wasted on
the impatient ears of youth.

"I'll call the DA… I don't know how we're gonna UN-
FUCK this monkey, but we're sure gonna TRY! Now
BEAT IT… and NO MORE 'proficiency tests. It's by
the book now, *YOU HEAR ME?"*

Three heads nodded as one. They got off cheap.
Sara practically sprinted from the room; that wasn't
her style. Her partner noticed, but her lover didn't. For
a stud, Eric was pretty naïve in the ways of women.
The two men headed down the hallway. Dunn spoke
softly to Sangreal.

"Wow… what's with Sarah?"
"I don't know… PMS maybe?"

Bill shook his head, then lowered his voice.

"I normally stay out of a man's love life, but this is an exception. I couldn't help noticing; whenever you say 'Kaylee,' my partner shoots daggers. A man can't ride with a partner long before he knows all the looks"

Eric stayed quiet as they walked down the hallway.

"I mean, we're men... We're bees; we pollinate some beautiful flowers... Now, I'm not askin' if you're dickin' that gorgeous little Parker babe or not. Can't say I'd blame you. All I'm sayin' is, you've got a great woman in Sarah. She's just learnin' to trust men again. If she WERE to find out about any uh... cross-pollinatin', it would wreak havoc. It would be worse for her than for other women, if you get my drift."

Eric's red-faced silence was a deafening confession.

"When I was your age, I was a swingin' dick too, with little care for the consequences. Hell, I thought my womanizing was something to be proud of. But later I learned the truth."

Actually, Dunn was only four years older than Eric, but it was the wrong time to mention it. Besides, he felt too guilty to refute it.

"This investigation won't be helped by the distraction an affair always causes. You see where I'm goin' with this, amigo? Keep your dick in your pants and help me keep this investigation from goin' any further south. What do ya say, brother?"

Eric could only nod; shame and lust commingled, conspiring against his larynx. He loved Sarah; she was loyal, smart and pretty. But in the sex department, she was cold and detached. Her idea of making love was to lie perfectly still until Eric got his nut. Then she'd peck him on the lips, jump out of bed and wash up without saying a word. It wasn't passion, it was protocol. Only recently had she let him fuck her in the shower… and even that was a mechanical procedure, not the hot-blooded, young lover shower sex it should have been. Could have been...

Then there was Kaylee, hot, consumed with lust. They were together just four minutes when they started tearing off clothes, screwing like teenagers, standing nude in the moonlight, her naked ass pressed against Beau and Duke's kennel, the two groaned and boned with unbridled passion. With her tight, muscular ass pressed against the cool wire, his hot body ramming her, Kaylee gasped at the sensory contrast. When he'd thrust, she'd moan and thrust back. And the wet, cold bloodhound noses touching her thighs and his balls... With the contrasting stimuli, full moon and new passion, it was incredible.

She invited him inside. Odd that her Jacuzzi was up to temperature and bubbling. Then it dawned on him; she'd planned it. The next two orgasms were shared in the Jacuzzi. After that he felt the raw ass scratches burning from spa chemicals,he went to get dressed while she kept calling him back.

A man can only fuck so much before he needs to recharge. With her jaw clenched in passionate determination, she got out, dripping foam from both nipples… just like Sarah had seen in her vodka-vision. The recharging could wait; they went at it again; soapy, slippery, right on the cherrywood floor kind of sex.

And now, the image faded; Bill nailed him cold. He wondered if Sarah knew, too. He made a note to hide his ass 'til the scratches healed... then another note, to get more of 'em... Damn, that woman could fuck; what a great flower to pollinate. The bee went to work, trying not to think about the future.

MISCONDUCT

Lt. Medaris wasn't exactly enthralled; three of his best kids went rogue on him. Normally, that was grounds for discipline, maybe transfers, but this wasn't a normal rogue op where somebody's lover needed a dead-beat dad's address or a wife-beater's ass kicked. It was a no-shit covert op, where his kids gill-netted a big-time shark. Now, if they could only get the thing back on top of the table, they'd nail a serial child killer. It was worth a shot; *fuck that...* it was worth a career.

Throughout his career he had seen plenty of assholes get off, due to flimsy loopholes and the sleaziest lawyering. Maybe it was time to make some loopholes for the good guys. If his posse had managed to take a few shortcuts, what the fuck; he'd back 'em if he could. He called the DA's private number. She saw the Caller ID and smiled a thin little cougar smile.
"De La Vega"
"John; gotta run somethin' big past you... buy ya lunch?"
She knew the guy needed to be off the record for this one. But then, didn't they all?
"Fargo's, eleven thirty; bring your wallet, honey."

The phone went dead before he could say goodbye. She always got right to the point. He liked her the first time he saw her. Half African-American, half Hispanic, in great shape, tall, trim, curves in all the right places. He felt a thrill inside. Then he hung up.

She was a formula car, built for speed, not comfort. She fucked like she prosecuted; brutal, to the point and goal-oriented. She went from zero to orgasm in sixty seconds.

But like most white-hot affairs, theirs barely lasted six months. She was a preying mantis, hunting for the ultimate lover. Medaris could still fuck like a young man, but his recharge time wasn't as great. He'd be a great fallback lover... if she ever needed one. So far, she hadn't.

So their relationship neutered. They became two ex-lovers, whose jobs forced them to act like they'd never wrinkled sheets. He was sage enough to accept; he was now a bench warmer.

Her job had lately taken on Atlantic proportions, which put a crimp in her sex life. Nowadays, orgasms were few and far between. The trade-off was her excellent conviction record, positioning her for a governor's campaign. If she won, she'd get to fuck everybody.

They met at Fargo's, the finest hotdog stand in Gander City. It moved every day, but always within a four-block radius of the courthouse, eliminating chances for eavesdroppers. Medaris had two chilidogs ready when she sat down on the concrete flower box.
"De La... You look good!"
She grabbed the proffered dog in its paperboard bowl and took a bite; loved talking with her mouth full.
"Hey, Dick; whassup?"
Good; the pet names still held; maybe some pollinating in the offing.
Medaris raised his eyebrows in curiosity.
"What would you say, *hypothetically speaking,* if my guys went rogue on me and managed to snag a serial killer?"

"OH, *honey*... don't toy with me!"

She almost had an orgasm; what a feather in her cap, just eleven months before tossing her hat in the ring.

"Are you for real?"

He swallowed a huge chunk of tube steak.

"Real as a fuckin' heart attack... But we have a couple cracks; I had to call you, De la."

Her mind swirled; a fuckin' serial killer... sonofabitch, she'd weld up all the cracks in the evidence chain. She'd weld the fuckin' Titanic hull, for this one.

"What *snags,* my man?"

He laid it out while her eyes bored holes through him. That look always got him hot. If there was one thing he liked more than her sexual vigor, it was her unrelenting concentration; she could focus like nobody he'd ever met. He disgorged the deal before asking her opinion.

"What do you think?"

"Well, it could work. Since your guys only recently heard of the first scent point, I'll bet a judge will grant a warrant. I mean, *they came to you with it right away,* right? Sounds like probable cause to me, honey. I'll go to the judge after he gets back from lunch, which by the way, for Hornyass, is three fifteen. To my way of thinking, that gives us three hours to burn... I'm horny as hell. Feel like playing hooky? Let's get a room."

The fallback sex wasn't bad, but it wasn't as good as either had fantasized about. After they showered and began dressing, Medaris' thoughts ran to The Honorable Judge Luther T. Hornhuis. The correct Dutch pronunciation sounded like "Horn House", but he got his nickname the old fashioned way;

He earned it.

During his early years, Hornyass biased many a ruling for the prettiest female. Not one to leave such bias merely on the bench, he took it into private chambers, trading many a favorable judgment under his robe. It took substantial complaints before the judicial affairs committee took him to task. They took it easy on him the first time, because most of the judges were guilty of far worse things than a little sexual extortion. Still, he'd have to dial down the gender bias... or else.

So he dialed it down until the heat died off. It was the second complaint that forced the board to officially sanction him, hence his tenure as a warrant judge, with a bit of capped insurance arbitration thrown into the mix.

"You think Hornyass will give us a warrant?"
She bent lithely for her left shoe.

"Probably. I bet I'll have to shake my ass for him, though. I don't know if I've got any sex appeal left; I think you just fucked it all outta me, babe!"

He snorted contemptuously while he watched her bend again for her right shoe.
"Bullshit… you've got enough left for sixty warrants."

She smiled; "Oh, yeah? Well you didn't do so bad either, for a wheezing old geezer. Call me sometime?"

The soon-to-be governor left as fast as she came.

Medaris lay back and sucked air, speaking out loud; "Damn, Johnny me boy... *you gotta get back in shape.*"

When he got back to his desk, an aide brought a note.
"Sir, this deputy called several times; she's on line three again right now."

He punched the button and got an ear full of sweet female cop voice.

"Deputy Baxter, Mendonesia Sheriff's Department …"
"Medaris here. What can I do for you, Baxter?"
"We have some remains; might be your missing girl, Tiffany Simpson."
"You need vitals?"
The deputy unconsciously nodded.
"That's right; not sure yet, but osteology and time frame's a match. Records & DNA would be helpful."

"You got it, Baxter!"
They exchanged contact info. He tried to call De La Vega next, but she was still shaking it for Hornyass.

Apparently she hit the right buttons; the warrant arrived before quitting time. Medaris could hardly wait to tell his rogues; their moth was ready for netting. He radioed Gonzales and Burke to come to the station... His instructions were best said in private. There were too many lawyers out there with police scanners.

They aborted their search of a chronic drug dealer; they could catch this asshole any time, and it sounded like the boss had something big cooking. They rolled into headquarters, while he walked over.

"Boys, remember that pervert, Sandoval? Maybe the asshole didn't do it. We got a new lead; here's the search warrant for David I. Eastbrook, 1900 block, Connestoga. You know the drill, but pay special attention to the RV; got a report of a hound pointing it. The hound's usual handler wasn't there and the dumb-ass civilian missed the point."

Burke confirmed; "You got it, boss."

They backed the unit out, but Medaris gestured.

"Oh, boys? Get Blisters and Jalapeno to back you up. Good hunting."

"Thanks, boss."

They started out when Medaris pulled his best Columbo impersonation; "*ONE MORE THING.*"

Medaris approached and spoke softly.

"*TRY* not to arrest this guy so hard... Tell Blisters and Jalapeno, I want him pretty for the media, *GOT IT?*"

They nodded and drove off.

"Shit; Lister & Jalapez had the fun, but *we* get heat."

Gonzales was stoic, as usual.

"Si, amigo, pero *this time...* we get the fun. Maybe we have a radio failure, 'n we have to bust this pervert alone. *Anything can happen, eh, compadre?*"

BUST

Just back from the final Texas pageant, a tired killer sat down, goblet of room temperature Petite Syrah in hand. His favorite porn site was just coming up. Pop-ups for various soft porn purchases for 'extremely young looking' adults teased him. He never clicked on those, knowing that some kind of supercop might be searching them, looking for perps like Eastbrook. Then he heard a crashing noise.

He instinctively knew it was his front door falling to a battering ram. The shocked pedophile turned off the computer. The screen started to fade; onrushing cops cascaded on him. His wine stained the carpet as the cuffs snapped closed. Gonzales spoke crisply.

"David Eastbrook, you're under arrest for the kidnap and murder of Tiffany Michelle Simpson. You have the right to remain silent…"

The rapist/killer blacked out from fear; or was it the fist to his temple? Burke cued the forensics dudes. The fun was over. Now the work began.

Cops crawled over Eastbrook's estate like maggots on a bloated cow, probing every nook and cranny. They pulled his laptops, hard drives, CDs, videotapes and all other electronics.

Eastbrook came to in the back seat of a squad car, feeling a bizarre mixture of pain, fear and closure. The cuffs, tightened to near-tourniquet specifications, provided exquisite pain, which traveled from the swelling wrists up the brachial afferents. Once the bilateral afferents joined in the cord, the impulses doubled in intensity.

He sat with his back pressing his wrists against the rough upholstery, scrubbing his naked forearms raw at every bump in the pavement.

His position was similar to those of his victims. In spite of his predicament, the thought of all those terrorized girls, arms pinned behind, made him sprout an erection and wish that he had a hand free to climax.

Beads of sweat formed on his swollen, bruised brow. The metallic taste of blood turned him on more; he fantasized it to be little Miss Arizona's blood; he spontaneously ejaculated. A tiny moan brought the words that would've gotten him killed, without Medaris' admonition to the contrary.

"You filthy bitch, Margaret…"

Burkey was driving and talking on the squawk box, so he missed the barely perceptible utterance. Gonzales had impeccable hearing; he swung his head around.

"Hey, partner, you hear this pervert? He say; "filthy bitch Margaret; Hey *LOOK… he came in his pants!"*

It was more exclamation than accusation. Gonzales never thought a man could come without at least having a hand on his dick. But then, he didn't know perverts. The wet stain showed front and center.

Burkey admonished quickly.

"Hey, we just *haul* the shit, we don't shovel it. And remember, Medaris said no resisting arrest this time."

So, unlike most pedophiles, he didn't manage to escape his cuffs, get out of the unit, fall on his face and box with the officers. They left the perp alone, cum-stained jeans, drool strands and all.

The rest of the drive back to HQ was uneventful.

MIRANDA

Due to the Sandoval incident, Medaris couldn't interrogate Eastbrook, but it was just as well; he just wanted to shoot the bastard twice through the head. Or once to the balls, then two to the head. Then, he'd dump the carcass in the desert, where scavengers could shred the rotting corpse. Hell, if it was good enough for his victims, it was more than good enough for this conscienceless predator.

Consequently, the interrogation honors fell to Commander Timothy Dockins. He was only too eager for it; he hated pedophiles and loved media attention. He walked into the interrogation room. The soft-spoken pedophile, chained to the steel bench, looked up. Dockins was surprised at how mild-mannered and meek the guy seemed.

"Mister Eastbrook? I'm Detective Tim Dockins... I'd like to first advise you of your charges and rights, if I may."

The killer nodded.
"Sure, go ahead."

Tim signaled to cue the digital recorder. He couldn't wait to rip this guy a new asshole. In an hour, he'd have him confessing to shooting JFK.

"You are under arrest for the kidnap and murder of Tiffany Michelle Simpson. You have the right to remain silent; anything you do say can and will be used against you in a court of law. You have the right to an attorney, before questioning. If you need an attorney and cannot afford one..."

The thing droned on, but hearing it again just made his head hurt more. The first time was enough, what with the knees in his back, knuckles to his temples and nightsticks to his torso. He knew his rights. Soon, the commander finished his little cop mantra.

"Do you understand these rights as I've read them to you?"
Eastbrook nodded.

"Please, speak up, so the microphone can get your response; do you understand these rights, as I've read them to you?"
His thick, swollen lips moved slightly, over three loose teeth.
"Yes, I understand them... I'm not *stupid,* you know."

Dockins instantly caught the chink in the armor.
"Oh, *I know you're not stupid.* It's just that... I have to read these to a lot of stupid people. But now that you understand your rights, would you like to waive 'em and just give me a confession right now? It might make you feel better to get it off your chest. Whaddyasay?"

Eastbrook had hung out with cops, but never could get over how stupid they were. To think he'd just confess; how dumb did they think he was? He scoffed.

"Yeah, *right*... I'm gonna *waive* my rights... you *must* think I'm stupid. What if I said I wanted a lawyer?"

Dockins was ready for the L word.
"Sure, that's your right. Here's a phone; it's on me."

He left and went inside the darkened cubicle behind the glass. A digital readout displayed the phone number; they knew it. A few minutes later, the suspect hung up. He smiled smugly; he was smarter than this cop, by a long shot.

Tim walked back in.
"So, are we good to go? You ready to confess? We can be having dinner, instead of sweatin' in here."

Eastbrook tried to deny the urge to purge, but somehow it seemed like it might ease his pain. He countered with another heavy ladling of sarcasm.
"Yeah, I'm gonna *waive* my rights and *confess;* I'm not stupid, you know..."
Tim loved to play stupid cop, a psychic can opener for snooty intellectuals; they could never wait to show off their superior brains.
"Well, David... or do you prefer Mister Eastbrook?"
The killer saw the ploy; again, with the sarcasm.
"Oh, call me Dave, Tim, I mean, we're off the record here, right?"

"Sure, Dave. I tell you what; I'll let you in on our evidence; you don't have to say a word. We've got a bloodhound pointing that girl's scent on your RV. You *DO remember*, with that big intellect of yours, when your buddy Darwin brought dogs to your place? They sniffed your drainpipe?"

The thought of the dogs knotted his guts. His forehead beaded with sweat.
"OH, and we've got hairs, Dave... "
Just then, the detective became aware of the soft

tapping on the glass, which kept getting louder; he got up impatiently.

"Excuse me; I need to confer with my... colleagues."

When the door closed, Eastbrook scoffed at the term. *Colleagues,* as if they were from Harvard; bunch of dumb-assed semi-moronic public servants. He was smarter than all of them combined.

Dockins hissed at his esteemed colleagues.
"What the hell you stoppin' me for?"
Medaris put a finger to his lips to hush him.

"You KNOW WHY! He asked for a fuckin' lawyer... You're ruinin' the whole fuckin' show."
Dockins answered in the same pissed-off whisper.
"The hell I can't! Weren't you listenin'? *Play the fuckin' tape back!"*

To be sure, they hadn't used tapes in decades, but old labels die hard; they replayed the digital recording while Tim lip-synched Eastbrook's words; *'Yeah, right... I'm gonna waive my rights...'*

"Now, I'm just a stupid cop; I don't know sarcasm, but it sounds to me like he waived his rights. All the parts are there! First, he dialed out for a lawyer; that's privileged, so I don't know if a lawyer's comin'...Then he waives his rights *again...* I vote for letting the lawyers sort it out, and get me the fuck back in there! He's ready to cave. A week's pay says I get him in an hour."

"Ok, you're on!"

He re-entered the interrogation room. He sat down; an aide came in and whispered in his ear. Eastbrook mentally scoffed at the cheap ploy.

"Oh, this is most interesting... Dave, what would you say if a couple of strands from your Winnemako matched that little Simpson girl?"

Eastbrook's eyes glazed and flickered with smoky delight, as mental pictures drifted; blond hair, cute little slit, hairless and squirming. She was so perfect.

Tim saw the eyelids flutter; the pervert was flashing back. He freshened the bait and opened the file.

"You remember Michelle?"
He recalled the fear in her sky-blue eyes; in spite of his predicament, he felt his loins stirring. Then the cop pulled out a studio shot of the little tattletale bitch. His mind started to fog.

"What made you pick her, Dave? Was she *special*? Did you stalk her first, to see if she'd qualify, Dave?"
Dockins picked up the photograph, so only he could see; a peep show, maybe... He slowed his speech rhythm to the fuck-beat that pedophiles love so much.

"OH she's a little young for me... but I can see why... you're so taken... with her..."

Tim's face aimed down, feigning looks at the photo, but he looked upward at his mark, hunting tells. Tim used the same trick at Poker. Eastbrook's legs rhythmically squirmed to the limits of the leg irons, rubbing his thighs against his scrotum and glans penis.

Tim had him literally by the nuts; he angled the photo so Eastbrook got a peek at the starlet. Then he turned up the heat.

"Well, she's... Oh, look at that *hair*... so pretty... isn't she?"

Eastbrook moaned involuntarily; strings of drool oozed from the corners of his mouth; if he could get just one finishing look at the bitch, he could have some release. He ground his thighs on his balls.

Dockins knew that pedophiles loved to dominate, terrorize and manipulate. He baited him some more.

"I'll bet she was *real* scared, those big blue eyes just rolling back... was she *scared, Dave?*"

He gave the perp a good peek, taking care to place his fingertips right over the tiny crotch. Eastbrook involuntarily shot his wad and blurted out bestially. "Filthy.... you filthy bitch, I killed you, *Margaret!'*

He nutted, timing it perfectly with '*Margaret.*' Then he came out of his fantasy, eyes lowered so the cop wouldn't see the tears of self-pity welling. The moronic cop just had him for lunch.

Tim was glad they made him leave his gun outside. Here was a pedophile, auto-ejaculating to the memory of a tortured, sodomized, murdered ten year-old kid... A pair of wadcutters through the temporal bones would solve the problem.

The only positive was getting it on record. His closure would come when he witnessed the execution, no matter how many years it took to kill the cocksucker. He forced his rage back under the badge; tough to do, but willpower was a prerequisite. He got up to go, but Eastbrook's voice turned surprisingly steely, stopping Tim in mid-stride.

"Oh, you think you're so smart, tricking me with your pictures of *ONE GIRL*... but if you knew how many there were, but you and your... '*colleagues*' never had a clue."

Tim felt his hatred being suddenly replaced with shock. Still, he never missed a chance to prompt. "How many were there, Dave? *How many?*"

Eastbrook raised his face; gone were the soft, momma-conning eyes. The viper's eyes were set firmly in the past, staring at unseen Margarets.

"It's about 176, but does it really matter? There's a river of them, like trout in a stream... Can you remember how many *trout* you caught? I started keeping souvenirs, to help me remember. I've been doing this a long time, Tim... And do you know something? You're right about me feeling better. I feel relieved already, just getting this one kill off my chest. Maybe I'll tell you more."

Dockins quickly assessed this new psyche; the Professor of Predation, eager to instruct semi-morons in the ways of abduction, torture and body dumping. It was surreal, but he took a lesson from Napoleon; *"When your enemy's making mistakes, don't interrupt."*

"You see, I have always had this... *affliction*; I'd just take one. Over time... I had to take them more frequently. Maybe I needed to be behind bars, but I got good enough, and taking them got so easy, it became hard to turn myself in."

The viper's eyes softened; he was coming out of his urge to purge. From years of interrogating suspects, Tim knew it spelled trouble. He took a shot at restarting the soliloquy.

"But... you *couldn't* hah? No more than a sane man can commit suicide."

No dice; the perp wasn't taking that bait, so Tim went back to little girls.

"So you stalked more of those long-haired, blonde girls with pretty blue eyes, didn't you? You like 'em *blonde... and blue... and young...* don't you?"

But the smooth-talking Eastbrook was back behind the eyes again; there was no calling the serpent back.

"Oh, Timothy; nice try, but I'm not taking that bait. We both know I'll never see the inside of a prison. You can't touch me, Detective."

As if on cue, noisy footsteps came down the hallway; in walked one of the most hated lawyers in the county. The officers had a derogatory nickname, thanks to such a careless appellation. For the record, he preferred "C. Paul Freely, Esquire" or failing that, C. Paul Freely, Attorney at Law... but *NEVER...* "Charles Pees Freely."

But by any name he knew the game. The cops booked 'em, Freely got 'em un-booked. Failing that, he got 'em off in court, and when a loss looked likely, he'd take a preemptive plea before seeing a courtroom. If the cops and prosecutors didn't like it, that was tough shit. He made his peace with the adversarial system a long time ago; had the townhouse and Ferrari to prove it.

He defended perverts with all the resources at his disposal, but after each case he'd vow to never represent a scumbag again. He even raised his fees to divert them to his less gifted colleagues. In a way, it almost worked. The excessive fees reduced contact with run of the mill scumbags, but paradoxically attracted affluent clients, who could feed their appetites in rare and exotic ways. Freely found himself trapped, defending the most elite pedophiles. Each case left a shittier taste in his mouth. It took a lot of Mimosas to wash the taste down.

Freely quickly tagged it; good cop seated, bad cop behind the glass. Defendant's tear-streaked, puffy face; dumb bastard looked like he'd been talking, in spite of the admonition to shut the hell up. The richer the pervert, the less they'd take his advice. He reached out his hand to shake the cop's hand.

"Glad to see you again, Detective…"

But cops *never* shook his hand; that never changed. Turning to the hidden camera behind the glass, he spoke louder.

"For the record, Charles Paul Freely, representing the accused, Mr. Eastbrook. I presume you Mirandized my client prior to questioning?"

Dockins smiled his cat-already-ate-the-Rotweiler smile; "Ah, but of course… we know the rules, counselor. I read them to him personally, and Mr. Eastbrook acknowledged; he understood his rights. It's all on tape, Counselor."

But the cop's smug smirk told the lawyer more.
"May I have a moment to confer with my client ?"
Dockins got up to leave, but Freely queried.
"OH, would it be too much to ask, to have the camera… *actually turned OFF?*"
The cop shrugged; the sleazy bastard was onto their tricks… fuckin' lawyers; he hated 'em all.

They turned off the camera, but not the microphones. It paid to one-up those defense lawyers whenever they could.

It wasn't Freely's first rodeo. He sat down, backside obliterating the camera. He brought out a small transistor radio. Tuning it to a country station, he set it down, speaker facing the microphones.

"Let 'em hear some C & W, eh? Cover your mouth like a major league pitcher, alright? Medaris is a fuckin' lip reader. Answer in whispers… Got it?"
Eastbrook covered and whispered "Got it"

"Good; ya got it already!"

The litigator opened his briefcase; "I'll talk you through while you sign tabbed areas… I get 80 thousand now, plus six hundred per hour for out of court work. IF we go to court, it's ten large per any part of a day, plus expenses & experts."
He watched his client like a long lost lover.
Eastbrook covered and whispered; "Ok"

The perp never twitched, so he must be loaded. Of course, Freely already did a credit check, but those could be manipulated. Better to eye his reaction firsthand.

"Now, these are very serious charges. Yours will be a MOST DIFFICULT case, as I'm sure you're aware. I must say; I'll have to double my usual fees, to have any chance of successfully defending you. This case could easily exceed 600 grand. Cool?"

Dave never hesitated; the huge fees actually made him feel more confident. He covered his mouth. One word hissed out.

"Cool."

With the documents and check signed, Freely relaxed. It wouldn't make him feel better, but at least he'd be well stocked in Mimosas. But if he any idea how many it might take to wash down the taste of defending this particular asshole, he would have quadrupled his fee.

"Obviously we can't discuss this fully, here and now, but I'm guessing from your appearance, you must have told them something... *what was it?*"

Eastbrook smiled weakly.
"Not much; I confessed, but they can't use it."

It was Freely's turn to itch for a sidearm; what was it about the rich? They always thought they were above the law; as if they could purchase or circumvent it.
"You're not kidding, *are you*?"

The rapist shrugged casually.
"I confessed, but *AFTER* I asked for a lawyer, so they can't use it... *can they?*"

Counselor Freely restrained his impulse to bitch-slap his new client; First he had to make sure his retainer cleared. He waived at the one-way glass. Thirty seconds later, Dockins sat across from the alleged scumbag and his hired snake.

"My client refuses to answer any more questions. Furthermore, I understand that you conducted an illegal interrogation *AFTER* my client asked for a lawyer. I'll be moving to have that suppressed. Lastly; unless you can provide evidence to the contrary, I'll be petitioning for an OR release. Judging from what I've HEARD, you have no grounds whatsoever to hold Mr. Eastbrook."

It was true; they didn't have much, aside from the confession, which wasn't exactly rock-solid. A lawyer this good could shoot it full of holes without reloading. Still, the game was afoot and they had his ass in a cell; possession is still nine - tenths of the law.

"Well, Counselor, we've got the vic's DNA in his vehicle. We've got a bloodhound that pointed his RV. We've got a search warrant. And unless I miss my mark, we've got him confessing to the whole thing…

 So you go and file your little motions. Meanwhile, Mr. Eastbrook dines with us tonight, and I hope he likes County Lockup Cuisine."

They got up to leave. The lawyer smelled a rat, but he let it go. He could always club the small rats later.

MOTIONS

Charles Pees Freely awoke, hung over, rubbed his temples and vowed again; the binges would have to stop. He stumbled into the shower. His late afternoon rally failed to get his client released. But then, he knew it would fail. Sex offenders or rather, *ALLEGED* sex offenders, never got a fair shake. Lady justice might be blind, but never naïve; the perverts would stay behind bars, pending the Second Coming of Christ.

He reached for shampoo, massaging it into his thinning scalp. The first order of business was to see that Eastbrook's check cleared. Then he'd have a proper sit-down. There were plenty of legal points to consider and motions to file. He rubbed the conditioner into his hair. While he was at it, a little went on his dick. It felt good, so he masturbated to the image of his new paralegal, Stefanie Walker. He couldn't wait to fuck her; had to be better than his hung-over shower-stall version.

Eastbrook had no priors. That alone was refreshing. However, it wouldn't make him any less culpable to a jury. They'd see another scum-of-the-earth, guilty-before-the-trial-starts pervert. But if that was Freely's biggest obstacle, it was also his biggest asset. He would turn their prejudice against them; a few would be honest enough to face it. One was all he needed.

Freely fired up his Ferrari and hauled ass for the office. Stefanie wasn't there yet, so he worked undistracted by the tight little Levi's. Sure enough, the check cleared. The lawyer grunted satisfactorily; his client was entitled to a thorough and vigorous defense. He surfed the client's website; he was relieved to see his client had a viable business.

The thumbnails were about church, support for peace officers, charities and so on. There was just one that bunched his guts in a knot. He reluctantly clicked on it. When it filled in, there was his client judging a pageant. He blurted aloud.
"FUCK ME... we're dead already."
"FUCK *WHOM*, counselor?"
He was so engrossed, he hadn't heard her enter.
"OH, Stefanie; sorry, I thought I was alone."

She shrugged and handed him coffee. Although she had only been with him for two months, this paralegal was one he could clearly trust.
"No problem; Let me guess; new pervert, same game?
"*Allegedly...* kidnap, rape and murder.
Stefanie cut the shit; "Did his retainer clear?"

"Yeah, we're good to go. The DA's going for the throat; dumb bastard *confessed.* It'll be tough to get it tossed... I'll do my best, but I'm sure he'll be getting the needle, about twelve years from now... unless some huge windfall saves him."
Stefanie filled in his unspoken thought.
"Yeah, right... and he could win the lotto, too."

He gathered his papers and called for a taxi; no way would his Testarosa see the jailhouse parking lot. Two minutes after Freely left, Stefanie was selling the story. This was why she'd shaken her ass for the chauvinistic prick in the first place; one good story and she'd be long gone; and this looked like the one.

CONFIDENTIAL

Presenting his ID, Charles Freely tried not to be annoyed at the frisking and briefcase search. It was understandable, since a local psychiatrist recently tried to smuggle a derringer to his incarcerated patient. The doc claimed that escape was in the best interest of his patient's mental health, and now it ws the shrink behind bars, hoping someone might bring him a derringer.

But while it didn't help the inmate's mental well-being, the shrink's bizarre act did plenty to heighten security. No longer did professionals get a breezy pass.

A buzzer sounded... the steel door unlocked; deputy and Freely stepped into a foyer. The lock slammed home. Freely never could get used to the sound. They were locked between two doors, five feet apart. The only furnishing, a tiny spy cam. A remote deputy searched them briefly; he could keep them there as long as he pleased. Seeing nothing unusual, the deputy buzzed and they opened the inner door.

The deputy led the way along the yellow line between rows of cells, each holding three to five stinking, screaming inmates. Many of them tried to hail Freely; they'd seen his TV and billboard ads. He waved his little Pope passing the peasants wave; he wouldn't be slowing down to absolve such lowly sinners, unless one of 'em won the lottery. Soon they came to the interrogation room. Deputy Dave Bear ensured it was free of contraband.

"So which scumbag are you here to free today?"
Freely raised a hand in mock objection.
"*ALLEGED* scumbag… *ALLEGED!*'"
He smiled his courtroom smile; Bear had none of it.
"David Eastbrook, s'il vous plait."

The burly deputy whisked away down the hall; for a big man, he could sure move… like his namesake. Images of a bear pouncing on a leaping salmon flooded his mind.

The tank held Eastbrook and two DUIs sleeping on the concrete in puddles of puke. Judging from the chunks, they both dined at the same greasy spoon.

"Eastbrook, your lawyer's here."
Bear hated perverts. He would love to take this one into a locked room and just interrogate his brains all over the walls, but he had four years left. He wasn't going to fuck it up. Besides, it wouldn't even begin to balance the scales.

Four more years and he'd be pensioned in Homer, jigging for halibut, drinking beer with his clan. North to the Future… Alaska and the good life. He walked the prisoner to the room, frisked him and shut the door.

Freely had more contracts to sign. He had his transistor out, tuned to the biggest heavy metal station in Gander City… So the cops bugged this room too. Either that or his lawyer took no chances.

"Mr. Eastbrook, your check cleared; congratulations, I'm your counsel. Here are a few more papers you need to sign."

Soon the pervert had signed away everything. Whatever his client had ever done or said, Freely could also be aware of it.

"Now, I'm not gonna bullshit you, Mr. Eastbrook."

"*Dave,* please... call me *Dave*, Mr. Freely."

"Ok, Dave, call me Chuck... but I'm not gonna bullshit you, Dave. Your case is virtually indefensible. You confessed... I can file a motion to have the confession tossed, but the judge that's gonna hear it... hared,y ever approves such a motion."

Eastbrook looked pained.

"But... But... I *asked for a lawyer*, just like on TV. Doesn't that negate whatever I said after that?"

Freely resisted the urge to belt him. He flashed back on Eastbrook's portfolio; IQ in the 160's, but dumber than a bag of hammers.

"Dave! Rule Number One; this is *REALITY!* TV tries to make you feel good about the legal system... But there's nothing about the law that makes *anybody feel good!* You've been charged with the worst crimes imaginable. You're the Boogie Man, every parent's worst nightmare. There's *NO WAY* you're going to get a fair trial; the interrogation is proof. The cops will do whatever it takes to send you to death row. They just don't give a fuck about rules!"

Eastbrook was blister-wrapped in denial. Freely had to peel off the façade before he could get his attention.

"Cops lie and cheat. They commit perjury, plant evidence and they'll sure as hell try to frame you! To the cops, *it's ALL GOOD,* if they nail you. Am I getting through to you, DAVE?"

The client appeared to be slowly coming around, so Freely kept up his jailhouse CPR.

"You know... They killed the last guy they arrested for this crime... *They fuckin' killed him!*

So it was true; they *DID* beat Sandoval. Recognition showed; Eastbrook was finally paying attention.

"OK, listen. I'll give you the rules. Follow them and you just might survive this thing. Rule number one; *DON'T TALK TO ANYBODY!* The walls have ears. Jailhouse snitches will do anything for less time or even just a day out to testify."

Eastbrook nodded.

"Rule number two; *DON'T LISTEN TO ANYBODY!* Lies, threats, misinformation are the People's tools of choice. If a cop, DA or inmate's lips are moving, they're lying... *YOU GOT THAT?"*

"Got it."

"Rule number three; *KEEP YOUR HEAD UP!* This will be a long war. You feel bad now? You'll feel worse later."

The lawyer came up for air. Eastbrook prompted him. "And rule number four?"

"Nope, just three; don't talk, don't listen and keep your head up. Now for the particulars... Tell me all about it."

The extreme serial pedophile finally let his hair down... In less than an hour, Freely learned more than wanted about stealing, raping, killing and burying young white girls. By the second hour, Charles Pees Freely knew there would NEVER be enough Mimosas to wash this one down... This monster was the granddaddy of all boogeymen.

Freely ended the conference on the third hour; he actually saw some options. If Eastbrook wasn't bullshitting him, one seemed to be solid gold. But then, clients had been known to lie before.

When he exited the jail, Charles was shocked to see a full panel of media-types. Microphones, cameras and anchorpersons rushed him. Questions cascaded in a deafening tumult. Obviously, someone leaked the story. One especially perky newswoman caught his eye; he chose to hear her above the din.

"Are you representing the ACCUSED?"

Freely loved publicity, but wasn't prepared for it.
"I represent Mr. Eastbrook. My name is C. Paul Freely; I don't have enough information to take questions… thank you, no further comment."

He forced through the press and leaped into a cab, headed for a destination where he could tell if Eastbrook was bullshitting him or not.

HACKERS

Freely knocked loudly on the door of the only place that would get him the truth. It took a few minutes before the occupant answered, since the blaring hip-hop all but obliterated the knuckle-raps. He entered the grungy apartment, with his arms full of truth-seeking equipment; hot pepperoni pizza and two packs of Red Cows.

Dan Sciacca, AKA Racer X, enthusiastically led him through the maze that once was a fine little living room. He steered him past an array of speakers, cables, scorched PC boards, half-dead flickering monitors and autopsied hard drives.

Dan cautioned Freely; don't step on the calico-camouflaged cat occupying the only empty spot on the rug. Sciacca swept a clear spot on the coffee table, while all sorts of crap hit the floor. Hot pizza was a priority. Besides, the floor wouldn't notice the extra trash; it was already three layers deep in taco wrappers, soda cans and micro-brew bottles. But what the kid lacked in housekeeping skills, he made up for with shear genius in cyber world.

Practiced hands opened the pizza box while he scanned the monitor; Pepperoni Braille while. Racer X was currently hacking into something of importance, but the lawyer was careful to *NOT see it;* a man could get disbarred if he knew of such crimes in progress. Sciacca pulled a slice and chomped half of it, all in one practiced motion; the kid would kill for hot pizza.

Racer X minimized the current clandestine pirating job and prepared for Freely's task. He wiped a greasy hand on his jeans and popped a Red Cow.

"So, what ya got for me this time, Chuck?"

Now it was the counselor's turn to hoist a slice of grease-dripping pizza. It would be rude to let the kid eat alone. Knowing how much he loved role-playing video games, he spoke in romantic parlance, using his best faux-Renassance dialect...

"I have a QUEST for you, my friend... You will be trussing the wings of justice. Mine client sits in the dungeon as we dine, accused of the most heinous crimes. It falls upon us to balance the scales of justice. I must warn you; should your search provide exonerating information, I might need you to come to the castle and testify in the King's court... D' accord?"

Sciacca's eyes glazed with lust. At last, his hacking skills might get him into the big time forensics arena. "Oh, *WAY COOL,* mon frere!"

"Bueno! My client's castle and computer have already been searched by the King's guards. At issue are certain files, already in the Dark Side's possession... There are uncontaminated original files, drifting in cyberspace. I need you to hack my client's system and find me the originals. Can you *do it?*"

Actually, Freely knew Dan could do it, but the lad could never resist a challenge.

"Oh, yeah... if they're out there I'll find 'em... What's his password?"

"*tattletale*."

Freely watched, slack-jawed, to see those greasy fingers fluttering. Perhaps pepperoni must lubricate keyboards. Before the pizza went cold, every single secret lay... exposed. It was frightening to see what thirty bucks' worth of fast food could buy. He was glad Racer X as an ally.

They forwarded the files to Freely's computer, relying on attorney client privilege to keep them secure... or at least, defensibly confidential.

Freely ended the visit by getting another vow of silence and promise to testify. Yes, he might call him as an expert. Yes, there would be a real paycheck in it... AND more Red Cow and pizza... Fuckin' unlimited pepperoni and Red Cow, if he got the client off.

He got up to leave; Dan was already back online, doing whatever it was that the lawyer shouldn't see. The defender of perverts drove home and went to bed early, trying to catch up on his sleep.

The was one small problem; for the first time since he started defending perverts, he was so excited he couldn't sleep. His thoughts hovered around the queries the press threw at him. One by one, the cascading queries floated back; they tumbled and dangled, in kaleidoscopic limbo. Even worse, he heard them as though they were all asked by that one pretty little brunette; the one they called Anchorpussy.

"Is it true he CONFESSED? Does he have a history of VIOLENCE? Will you try an insanity defense?"

He tossed and turned until the wee small hours. He got up and watched mind numbing informercials. He drank booze and took sleeping pills. He tried to recite dullest parts of the penal code. Nothing helped. What he'd discovered at Sciacca's was too earth shattering; he had the People by their collective balls.

He gave up on sleep and went to work at five AM.

Freely wouldn't show his cards too soon... It was risky; it could even get him disbarred, but it might be worth the risk. He called the jailhouse to see Eastbrook.

LOCKUP

The pedophile's normally quick mind went rusty-dull, inside the cell. He had two cellmates; scum of the earth meth dealers, twitchy little rats, whose only interests lay in self-destructive, short term gratification. Neither of them used a toothbrush or soap.

Ironically, they were the best roommates any pedophile could hope for. With any other cellmate, Eastbrook might already be dead. Even the hardest convicts had a code of honor about kids.

Gradually, the reality soaked in; a cop with semi-moronic IQ had tricked him... the long arm of the law knows nothing of witticism or sarcasm. Cops took every word literally, all the way to the witness stand.

He knew little of Freely, other than what he'd seen on billboards and TV. But after the first conference he felt better. Then, after another night in lockup, his confidence sagged. Just as the urge to chat with his cellmates overtook him, the deputy walked up.

"Eastbrook; your snake's here."

To deputy Bart Pepper, all lawyers were snakes; some just lived under fancier rocks. It never occurred to him that defense lawyers were a necessary part of the adversarial system.

For that to happen, Pepper would have to be arrested. He walked back to his station to do whatever he did when he wasn't messing with inmates.

Eastbrook heard the door locks buzz down the hall. Soon Chuck walked in, after being searched. He sat down and turned the radio on.

"Dave, I have some good news, BUT I don't want you sharing it, alright?"

"Yeah."

"We got your originals and copied 'em to my system... It's our ace in the hole; don't blab to anyone. Got it?"

"Got it."

"OK, next issue; I'm not going to move to suppress your confession. I know we talked about it, but this new evidence changes my strategy."

He hunched closer to his client.

"Now, regarding your other...actions; this changes our strategy... It's no longer just about *this case*. It's also about how the media impacts the families of past victims... The bigger this gets, the harder it will be to defend you."

David's face was stone.

"If I were to file the motions right now, they'd probably be granted. But the People are sniffing; it's just a matter of time before they find fresh, unimpeachable evidence... and we'll lose; I'M SURE OF IT!"

Signifying a change of tack, Freely raised a hand.

"On the other hand, IF we take our chances with trial *right now*... we can drop our bombs. Then when the dust settles, I'll file a motion to dismiss with prejudice. Do you know what that means? They can't retry you... you'll be off the hook... *for the Simpson case.*"

"Completely off the hook?"

"Yep, and the People couldn't use that information against you in other cases, either. Given the facts about your lifestyle, it's your only chance to dodge the needle."

The client looked pale; trickles of sweat slithered down his pasty face. To hear his lawyer talking about lethal injection was less than optimistic.

"OK, Chuck, whatever you say. I trust your judgment."

He still looked worried. Chuck read his mind.

"As for future trials, we'll cross those bridges later. Confidentially, the fact that you've never been arrested suggests you haven't left many clues. Prosecutors need solid evidence to try cold cases... it's a budget thing. I see you've lived all along the Bible Belt. Most poor counties lack the funds to go fishing in old cases, especially those opening church closets. Still, somewhere in your past lurks a prosecutor that will come for you. If it were me, I'd wait until I could pounce, like a cat on a mouse."

Eastbrook looked surprised at Freely's predatory words, which shouldn't come from a man's defense lawyer. Freely saw the look.

"Yeah, I was a prosecutor. I know all their chickenshit tricks, too... and I don't have a problem turning the tables. Some of the shit they pull is *unbelievable.*"

Freely packed up to leave. The guard searched them both. He walked the yellow line, through the double-doors of doom and out of jail.

Again the press was waiting. Anchorpussy was nowhere to be seen; maybe she couldn't get her petite little frame through the slob-mob. Too bad. She was pretty on TV but in person? Drop-dead gorgeous.

Seeing their shark emerge, the media swarmed him. He held up his hand and surprisingly, they went silent.

"I am C. Paul Freely, Attorney for Dave Eastbrook. I'll make a statement, but won't take questions... as my client's CONCERNS for a fair trial must come first."

He liked that statement going over the airways; it always netted him new clients.

"First of all, my client is ABSOLUTELY INNOCENT. Mr. Eastbrook is a HIGHLY REGARDED PILLAR of society, with NO PRIOR RECORD WHATSOEVER. He gives willingly to benevolent organizations and charities... He is a good guy, UNJUSTLY charged with a heinous crime."

He closed his hand closed into a podium-pounding fist.

"FURTHERMORE, once I succeed in defending him, I trust YOU will proclaim his innocence with the SAME VIGOR that you now *VILLIFY* HIM! Thank you."

He turned to leave; two microphones bumped his face.

"No comment.... Thank you."

The cameras recorded him getting into the cab... where he was finally free to think his own thoughts.

Of all the media queries, two repeatedly stung; *"Is it true he's a serial killer? Is it true he's done this before?"* He had no idea how the press dredged that up. If he hadn't been so engrossed, the answer would have scratched him in the face.

When Stefanie knew something, the press knew it. With this scoop, she'd have enough money to hit the road; Las Vegas it would be, while she still had the tits and ass to be a top-billing showgirl. The only reason she hired on with this defender of scum was to exploit just such a case. As far as she cared, Eastbrook was just one more pig at the trough; as guilty as a man could be... *IF* he got the needle, it would be too good for him.

If Stefanie had her say, every pedophile would be chained naked in a room, the victim's relatives free to extract their justice. A short list of tools topped her list; blowtorch, pliers, golf clubs... That wouldn't be torture enough, but it would be closer to what he deserved than a painless needle journey to a final sweet sleep.

Before the case would go stale, Stefanie would cash and walk. That was her specialty; a little ass shaking, a few dimple-punctuated giggles and men just opened their wallets. The fact that she fucked more than a few was just icing on the cake. According to her plan, Freely might be the last cake she'd have to ice, Then off to the big tents. She would be a star.

ANCHORPUSSY

Cathy O wrapped, stowing her mike in the bag. She got in the van and shrieked at Kevin, her cameraman.

"Fuck! I couldn't get through! We didn't get *anything* we could use! Six and Two will catch up with us!"

She was the sexiest anchorwoman-turned-reporter. Her ratings were tops for her slot. But it wasn't enough, not by a long shot. Mildred Agatha Percival wasn't content to be just another cutie-pie reporter... She wanted to be the next superstar, complete with talk show, endorsements, trophy men and a nine-figure net worth before she was thirty.

Her plan required perseverance and untethered greed; full speed ahead and damn the holdfasts. So she changed her name to Cathy O, something the masses could remember, if not spell.

Then came the cones, plastic surgery, caps, cardio classes, tanning, voice lessons, video coaching, and facial exercises ad nauseum. She was a rocket ship headed for the troposphere. There were talks of syndication.

But if she'd learned anything about TV land... talk's cheap. To grease the deal, Cathy O needed a super-scoop; a story like the Eastbrook-Simpson saga. It had all the ingredients, including a rich defendant. The masses loved to see rich people in the hot seat.

More importantly, the victim was The Great American Dream or at least, its first rapid eye movements; blonde, blue, lanky, photogenic. Her mother was a single mom, trying to make things better for her kid, in spite of a dead beat dad and other speed bumps.

To cap it off, Tiffany was taken in broad daylight, on a public street with forty people that didn't see a thing. The American Dream morphed into the Nightmare.

Stories like this were career makers; Cathy O would reap the rewards during syndication negotiation. But the damned defense lawyer wouldn't toss her a bone.

She kept shrieking at her cameraman… as if it would help. Kevin tried to calm her down.

"Oh, baby… take it easy; what did you *EXPECT* him to say; *'I think my client DID IT?'* We'll get him… YOU always get your man, Baby!"

Cathy O excelled in seducing truth out of men; part of her job description. That, plus bribing underlings; it took only two dirty Martinis to lubricate the selfish bitch. Cash swapped palms and the greedy paralegal shamelessly disgorged details.

But she hated to have information spoon-fed. It usually arrived a moment too late for proper exploitation. Then, it bothered her to have to actually *PAY* for the goods; far better if she could just flirt it out of a man. And, unless she missed the look, C. Paul Freely looked ripe for the procedure.

Her second meeting with Stefanie Walker paid off handsomely. She learned where Charles Pees Freely ate, drank, and who he slept with. Stefanie hadn't yet, but she was the exception. The man was a total hound.

She answered Kevin idly while daydreaming.

"Yeah… I *always nail 'em*, don't I?"

Her thoughts ran to the 'when and where' of the nailing while they drove to the next scoop; a kid took four pipe bombs to school, forcing evacuation and bomb squad; same shit, different school. The only good thing about such tiny crimes? They kept her on camera.

SEDUCTION

The Simpson case mesmerized the public. The media hounded prosecutor and defense for scraps. Cathy O led the pack, but felt her lead eroding. She could hear her syndication phone not ringing; if she didn't scoop this story soon, her career was over.

She caught up with him at Trevor's. He sat at the massive mahogany bar, facing a huge wall-length mirror. High above, the centerpiece scorned the open-beamed lodge; a dusty shoulder-mount Cape Buffalo sneered through squinted, angry glass eyes. Even in death, it looked pissed off.

Cathy O never could see the stuffed animal thing, but this one's bulk alone admittedly made an impressive statement. Surrounding the buff were vintage photos and artifacts from a bygone era. Blackpowder English double rifles, possibles bags, monocles and hand carved seven-foot shooting sticks finished off the motif. Give a man enough gin and tonic and he could smell the Veldt.

Three gimlet glasses lined the dark wood. Two were empty and the last was half-full or half-empty, depending on life philosophy. For Freely, it was half-drank; as soon as the world stopped spinning, he'd finish the task. He barely noticed the sexy brunette; man, *THAT'S* drunk.

Anchorpussy took a long, studious look; he was thirty-something, going on sixty. The dark sideburns had a few grays in the mix. His hands were clean and free of jewelry, save for one obnoxiously large gold and diamond entanglement, obviously there to impress bar whores, but it still didn't fit the man.

His face bore vestiges of chronic professional strain; tightness in the jaw, pursed lips, from biting off damaging words before they were spoken in court. His brow was deeply furrowed from years of reading law.

His arms once held strength; college boxer, wrestler maybe, but now the guns were empty shells. The heaviest thing they'd lifted in ten years had to be the California Penal Code.

He swung his head around, and for a short moment he looked like a miniature Cape Buffalo; dull, pissed off squinty eyes, pointing at her. All he lacked was the black horn boss.

It took a second for Cathy O to get his tell; freeing scumbags, so they could do ugly things to more innocent kids. She figured how to seduce his truth. She shook her locks and flashed her killer smile.

"Buy a girl a drink, cowboy?"

He grunted, gave the barkeep a fifty while she ordered.

"Screwdriver for me, and another gimlet, kind sir."

The Barkeep smiled; "Me name's Barnie, m'lady."

She muttered to herself; *Again with the African motif... what's next, a Masai spear?'*

The lawyer's eyes softened, absorbing her beauty; "What *you doin' here*, Anchorpu... I mean; Cathy O?"

"It's OK. Call me Anchorpussy; as long as you accentuate the last two syllables... Key word, *believe me...*"

If there was one thing he liked, it was a woman brave enough to be direct with sexuality. The drinks came and she sucked down the top half of her screwdriver before gasping for air.

"Damn, that tastes great! Nothing like a good belt to wash down the taste! God, I *HATE* covering stories on perverts; makes my skin crawl."

He parried the cheap attempt at fraternization. Frankly, he thought she had more brains than to try such a cheap ploy. Who the fuck did she think she was, trying to outsmart him... a trial lawyer, for chrissakes. Still, she was cute as hell; may as well put a carrot on the string.

"HUH? *YOU* hate 'em? You oughta try defendin' 'em."

She slid her stool closer; her right breast accidentally brushed his left shoulder. Two more rounds and a dozen breast accidents later, her magic worked.

Anchorpussy used reverse psychology; they swore NOT to discuss the case. Then she acted bored when the convo went elsewhere. The world's most pussy-whipped trial lawyer started spilling his guts. Yes, he hated defending perverts, but somebody had to do it. It's why he charged so much and drank so much.

It's also why her left hand rested firmly on his dick by last call. They went to his place. He finally nailed Anchorpussy... But it was mutual. The day's breaking story got Cathy O her syndication deal. The story aired all across the nation; including Yuma. She kept the morning spot vague, cock-teasing the audience so they'd watch later. She flaunted tidbits to show that she alone had the inside track on the trial.

The morning scoop ended as he awoke; a river of gimlets, jiggling breasts and wild sex formed a dim, pagan collage. He wasn't sure; it might have been Anchorpussy in his bed last night. He smelled the pillow. Olfaction confirmed it; the sneaky bitch worked her sweet evil magic on him.

He got into the shower and the worrying began; not able to recall precisely what he told her, one word kept battering his hung-over brain; *DISBARMENT.* If he told her anything and his client found out, one phone call from his disgruntled client could end Freely's career.

Then too, the Prosecution could turn him in. Or any lawyer-hating cop could drop a dime if they learned of the breach. And Cathy O; she could use his ethics breach to leverage more details in the future.

By the time he finished dressing, he worked through the what-ifs... and disbarment didn't sound so bad. His conscience had been getting harder to ignore, after each pedophile he defended.

He hopped into his car and it growled to life. Gunning the Ferrari to redline, Freely burned rubber and hauled ass; nothing can salve a man's pain like the tenor roar of a Testarosa. He decided on the way; he had one last scumbag to free. After that? He'd take a monster Sabbatical.

TRIAL

California V. Eastbrook quickly materialized, due in no small part to the pedophile factor. It was also due to Freely's hastening the process as much as possible; speed fostered errors.

The arraignment went OK, with just four words coming from his hotshot lawyer; *"Not Guilty, your honor."* It didn't seem like much, considering the monster fees, but he learned one thing in business; hire the best... Then, let 'em work.

Every face in the courthouse eyed him with hatred. He was the bug in the jar. They were the mean little kids that *might* poke a few air holes in the lid.

Try as he might, he couldn't understand their hatred. Sure, he'd raped some girls, but they got what they deserved, the momma-squealing, tattle-tail bitches. It wasn't like he was evil... he just had an affliction, and fortunately the cure was quite pleasant; find a perfect mark, scare her and rape her. Of course, then he had to kill them, so they wouldn't tattle. But what was the bid deal? There was a river of girls out there. He only took what he needed; it was puzzling, why others took offense over something so trivial.

His days in lockup gave him time to ponder the conundrum. At counsel's request, Eastbrook was in solitary to prevent inmates from killing him. His days were a mind numbing routine; eat, sleep and wait. Being a creative type, he found a way to pass the time. He masturbated to the memories of his victims. It wasn't as good without his videos and trophies, but it still helped.

INTEROGATORIES

The rapist studied the first wave filing the gallery; they looked nervous. Some looked perturbed. Every one of them looked at him sooner or later. The look was always the same; he was dead meat.

"Chuck... is that all of the prospective jurors?"

"No. We've got hundreds waiting in the wings. Just remember what I told you about the interrogatories."

Chuck and the Prosecutor drafted questions, posed them to the judge, and then argued compromises. The first section held vitals; age, sex, location, occupation, marital status.

The next section probed the issue of religion; would they deliberate on god's or man's law? The lawyers wanted to know if their work might get wasted on one stupid housewife stubbornly sticking with god's greater scheme, instead of the facts in evidence. Many a trial has hung for such conflicts.

The next section dealt with the death penalty; the prosecution couldn't wait to stick the needle in his arm. Even those who didn't like the needle saw this as the exception; if it should go into *anyone's arm,* it sure as hell ought to be *Eastbrook's.*

The defense opposed. Lethal injection was cruel, unusual and irreversible; and since DNA has exonerated hundreds of wrongfully convicted killers, reversibility seemed a good thing to keep in the mix.

The next section probed juror's sex lives. Were they gay, straight, swingers or swappers? These were just softening-up, foreplay queries for the increasingly weirder questions; did they view soft porn, how often, please check which kinks applied; threesomes, orgies, films showing erect penises going into traditional orifices... So far, just normal fucking and fantasizing.

Then the shit got weirder. please check; condoms, ribbed, colored, vibrators, masturbatory aids, blow-up dolls, dildos, strap-ons, cock rings, anal beads, edible undergarments, body sauces.

For the most persevering applicants, the list went on, but most of the straight panel stopped checking boxes way, way back near condoms.

The subsequent section asked about cross-dressing, costuming, use of feathers as opposed to the whole chicken, sadomasochism, dominatrix games and peep shows. Had they ever engaged in sex acts where pain was deliberately inflicted? Had they performed choke-sex to heighten orgasm?

From there it was but a few lines to the hard core questions the lawyers really wanted answered; had they ever been aroused by photos of a nude child or while observing a child urinate, defecate or vomit?

For a few applicants, the sex interrogatory didn't go far enough, but what could one expect from two straight thinking lawyers and a hetero judge?

But just when the queries were certain to alienate every applicant, the next section showed why they'd been asked... If they heard such evidence, could they keep an impartial mind and weigh all the facts?

By the end of the questionnaire, the jury pool felt like they went through a surgical operation... exhausted and disillusioned, they had to come back a week later, giving the court time to scan the interrogatories.

One week later, the dog and pony show set up their tent. The first twelve were sworn in. The prosecution shuffled interrogatories, busily linking papers to faces. They wanted jurors that would stick the needle in his arm; god-fearing, salt of the earth straight-sex, eye-for-an-eye churchgoers, ideally who lost a child. Grief drives 'em extra miles to the execution viewing room.

Charles Pees Freely wanted *HIS jurors* YOUNG. Raging hormones defy reasoned argument. True, it was a huge leap from sexual license to outright pedophilia; but young legs leap furthest.

His ideal juror was out of work, had tattoos, unconventional hairdos. And, while body piercing wasn't allowed in court, he would keep a keen eye out. Extra stars went to kids into Goth, violent video games, cults and, although it would be too much to hope for, outright necrophilia.

The People's consultant whispered into De La Vega's left ear. The expert was paid for by a special fund whose sole purpose was to convict pedophiles. It was your basic poker game, to guess juror's minds based on appearance, posture and the interrogatory.

Eastbrook thought back on what Freely said about consultants; *'They don't know shit.'* To try to know the heart by looking at the outward body... Was pure folly. The pedophile scoffed at the thought; if he were in the box, the consultant might think that Eastbrook was the perfect juror.

Meanwhile, Charles Freely had no such hired gun. He had seen too many surprising verdicts to put much credence in specialists. He went with his head and gut. His minimalist approach worked as well as anything.

SELECTION

Most people cited time away from work, school or vacations. There were religious excuses. Of course, prospects specified this on the last page of the interrogatory; it would've been faster to have the lawyers read them first and then excuse, but the law calls for each one to go on record.

So, two hundred prospects sat in the basement like canned herrings. Some were called up three stories to the courtroom, to sit and wait to be called into the box; then Court turned its microscope on that person.

The basement pool had the best of it; they got to watch a video proclaiming how vital jurors were; the film omitted the fact that many trials don't use juries at all, but we won't go there right now.

Then after the film ended, the clerk instructed the basement clan in less lofty issues; they had to park six blocks away. The meter maid would cite expired meters. They wouldn't be paid for the first three days, but if it went longer, they'd get ten bucks per day, plus one-way mileage.

So there it was, for all to try to pretend otherwise; the juror was making ten greenbacks a day, minus parking, lunch and daycare... But jurors were so very important to the judicial process.

Amazing, to think they could ever get twelve people in the box.

And so, wave by wave, they took the oath, sat down and got dismissed; but there was the occasional juror ripe for picking. Finally, Eastbrook had his jury of peers; fourteen people who were either too stupid or too unimaginative to get out of jury duty. So much for peers. He lost nerve. He smiled a nervous little smile.

"What if something goes wrong, Chuck?"

Freely hated that smile; it was for conning moms out of their daughters. He wanted to hit him with a face-crunching right cross. It had been a long time since he'd seen teeth chicklets scatter across hardwood, but now seemed like a good time for it. Instead, he had to represent the bastard."Then we'll go to plan B... we'll gut it out, grind it out and dig at every chink in the state's armor."

The killer didn't look confident, so Freely revisited it during recess.

"The People will show gory photos. I won't be able to keep 'em out, so instead, I'll keep them in front of the jury, every hour of every day, unless the prosecution objects. If I can keep the pictures up, we'll be ok."

"It sounds weird, but desensitization has worked before... All it takes is plenty of stare-time. Believe me, they'll get bored; they can't help it... The state will bring a forensic entomologist, a glorified bug counter. He'll try to shock 'em; maggots crawling on poor little Shelly, shit like that. Again, if it's brief, it *WILL convict you*."

"But then I'll bring in *MY EXPERTS*; believe me, they can talk maggots until the whole fucking court falls asleep. We'll have maggot consumption pie charts, blow-ups of maggot life cycles, charts for other bugs... the whole works! When we finish arguing third instars, hide beetles and parasitoids for two weeks, the jury will be comatose; the longer we talk bugs, the less they'll care that bugs were eating your victim. Sorry; *'alleged victim'*.

Eastbrook still looked unsure.

"Do you know what I like about battles of the experts? *I always win!* The state hires one expert; we hire three. The state hires low bidder, so we hire the best. When experts battle, they *BAFFLE.*"

"You really think so?"

"Yeah... I know the state's bug man. He's good with bugs, but he's a horrible witness. He can talk a jury right into a coma. Besides, his data is conviction-oriented; I'll open him up like a can of Spam."

"He'll try to bullshit the jury about TOD, based upon standard rate of insect progression; we're talking flies, basically. He'll try to convince them the cycle is carved in stone, but it depends upon how many sun-hours and degree-days and shit like that."

"So?"

"So, in order to make a *FORENSICALLY ACCURATE time of death* based on maggot progression, you can't fuck around. You have to set up a weather station at the crime scene and gather data. Then you compare that to standard weather patterns before you can say with forensic certainty how many instar cycles have elapsed... *AT THE SCENE.*"

"Wow... But..."

"Without using the weather station, the bug man's guessing... and when *I'M* crossing him, guessing won't be good enough. So, once I rip their expert a new ass, we'll have a juror in our pockets. After the experts bore the jury to tears, the only ones who will still care about the victim will be her relatives. It's all about desensitizing jurors; if we can do that, we're halfway to acquittal or a mistrial at worst."

The accused started to look more confident.

"We have other chinks; I'm gonna attack every fucking one. That's why you hired me; attack, attack, *attack!* "

Chuck was in the zone, fueled by his own words.

"Some people hate the government spying on citizens. Maybe one hates it enough to throw you a bone. There was a deep canyon where the satellite lost the jeep signal... maybe it got wet crossing a stream, but the RFID quit working THREE MILES from the grave site. It's reason enough, for any juror looking to acquit. Throw enough doubt bones; maybe one dog starts chewing. Remember the six basic defenses...

I didn't do it... I didn't know I did it... I didn't mean to do it... I had to do it. Somebody MADE ME DO IT... Somebody else did it?"

"Yes, I remember"

"Well, that other guy, Sandoval? The deceased's DNA was in *HIS* car. Then he *mysteriously dies IN CUSTODY*... now, *that guy* was into boys, not girls, but I can still spin it our way... and I'll use the People's own words to do it."

"You see, it's very difficult to profile a sexual predator; The California Penal Code says so, and so does the DOJ website, and I'm gonna cite both... After that, who's the jury gonna go with; Sandoval or a solid citizen with no criminal record? Which man fits the image of a rapist?"

"That should get us a juror or two. Meanwhile, the cops and DA are drifting toward Niagara Falls, back-paddling for all they're worth. We'll present police brutality, malicious prosecution and tainted evidence. With the right breaks, we can get an acquittal."

"You think so?"

"Yeah, I do. Now my '*WHAT IF'* speech is complete; I'll desensitize, point blame and cast doubt. If you sling enough shit, some is bound to stick.

"Besides that, I know a few goodies about the prosecutor and a certain cop; I've been saving it for a rainy day. if I have to, I'll sling some shit their way. But most of all, I'm still hoping we get the case tossed... You *do remember* plan A?"

Eastbrook nodded and smiled weakly; "Yes"

"Good! Keep your mouth shut and your chin up!"

He called for the guards to take the killer back to jail.

I mean... *ALLEGED   killer.*

REFLECTION

He never liked how he felt after speaking with pedophiles. He sat in the bar, studying the ice cubes melting in his Scotch, replaying the talk he'd just had with his worst-ever scumbag.

He inventoried the smoking guns he hadn't mentioned to his client; if he couldn't get the evidence tossed, he didn't have a clue how to defend those items, such as; victim's blood, feces and epithelials smeared all over the plastic vacuum cone. Freely's ass hurt at the thought of the kid's pain. For that alone, he wanted to kill Eastbrook, not defend him.

The piece of polycarbonate was more than a smoking gun; it was the USS MISSOURI'S Blackpowder bores firing boulder-sized ordnance twenty miles onto some South Pacific atoll. If the cone got in evidence, his client was up-the-ass-dead.

Then it didn't seem like such a bad idea, really, the tapered cone legally raping Eastbrook, just like he had raped so many girls with it. Freely loved the irony.

He ordered another; the booze started to hit him, and so did the idea he'd been trying to dodge; there had to be more to life than defending assholes like Eastbrook.

In a way, he preferred his life back when he prosecuted. And, except for a few innocent men that he convicted, Freely enjoyed his prosecuting phase. But with knowledge comes pain. Convicting innocent men tasted slightly worse than setting perverts free.

Only now, at the azimuth of his career, Charles Pees Freely felt the moral cataracts forming... he'd seen too much ugly shit on both sides of the legal fence, and that was the gods' honest truth of it.

Back in law school, neither side had yet to singe his idealism. He had big plans; he would graduate and he would wield the legal saber, slay some dragons, win fair maidens and drink the king's grog.

But none of it came true. The dragons were corporate fire breathers, with gangs of lawyers guarding their caves. Against dragons that huge, a mere knight wouldn't suffice no matter how pure his heart was.

The wrongs could never be righted, the defendants too guilty and despicable. And the maidens? Most had been anything BUT fair; cunning and laden with hidden agendas, he never could tell who was screwing whom.

It began to dawn on him around the next Scotch, that Karma was at work. His self-inflated, testosterone poisoned lifestyle was probably to blame for it all.

He thought back, with the clarity of the drunken philosopher... To a time when he had a shot at a different life. Back then, scouts ogled his 90-mile per hour fastball, but they drooled at his knuckler.

Chucky Freely had an eighty mile per hour knuckle ball that moved three feet in the last five yards before the plate. Nobody could hit it. He had three state championship rings to prove it. He won a four-year ride with that UN-hittable knuckler.

But then, pussy entered the picture. Selena was seventeen, with the biggest, tightest tits young Chucky had ever seen. Before he knew it he flunked out; *FUCKED his way out,* would be more like it.

Selena and Chucky fucked all day and night, week in, week out. Hormones, pheromones and sex moans bounced off the sheetrock.

When they weren't screwing, they were eating, drinking and replenishing, so they could fuck some more. They groaned and moaned and boned for damned near a year straight, while Freely never threw a fastball or knuckleball; he was too busy playing with his other two balls.

The lawyer finished his drink and started walking. He was glad he left the Ferrari home. Besides, he wanted to think about Selena; It had been a long time since he'd savored the sweet memories.

Then it struck him; they made love for a year straight, without tiring of each other. What a remarkable achievement; never would he find that again, try though he might. So he walked and reminisced.

Then one day, Selena moved to Europe. The young stud stood there with his dick in his hand and nowhere to put it. The pheromone stupor wore off; the phone wasn't ringing, the scouts weren't calling. The revoked scholarship would never be on the table again... his window of opportunity got painted shut, but he had been too sexually stupefied to smell the paint drying.

He cringed at the thought of a suboptimal future, but he adapted fast. Freely worked days and went to school nights. Only rarely did he look back; he traded his future for a year of unbridled lust. Not a bad trade, but surely an irreversible one.

But the worst part? He still missed Selena, so many years and lovers later.

Freely pondered how many men screwed themselves out of great futures, thanks to the carnal trilogy; sex, drugs and booze. A phrase from Desiderata hit him...

'N*othing is more common than*

unsuccessful men with talent."

Perhaps that was the main difference between plumber and pro pitcher; the former engaged distraction, the latter dodged it.

Perhaps it was just about sin, seduction and weapons of mass distraction, and a young man's limited capacity to evade these mortal pitfalls. Maybe every kid had big league talent, which was covered up by distraction and sin. Who the fuck knows?

A lawyer defending sinners, that's who! Hell, if anyone should, Charles Pees Freely sure as hell ought to.

He stumbled on this truth as he stumbled up his stairs.

He fumbled for his keys. Suddenly a vagrant whiff of perfume came to his nostrils. His thoughts turned to Anchorpussy; odd that a man only recalls his first and last piece of ass. The rest is merely filler. With any luck, his next piece was heating up in his Jacuzzi. He opened the door to find out.

OPENERS

The lawyers were seated. Jurors took their seats. The gallery filled with spectators, including Cathy O's crew, Taking care to set up in their designated position, as per His Honor's instructions.

There was to be no parabolic eavesdropping, no shots of the jury, and only cameos of the lawyers. He was tired of ambulance-chasing lawyers grandstanding, pulling cheap histrionics for free airtime. But mostly, Judge Ray was tired of having the flaws of justice exposed on TV. He loved the law, even its quirky loopholes and exotic provisos. To have lay people autopsy them was too offensive; it was trailer trash critiquing the Mona Lisa; it pissed him off.

Cathy O wanted a clean shot of De La Vega giving her opener, but getting it, without shooting a juror's face took some finessing. Fortunately, the judge allowed them to rehearse on Saturday. De La eagerly complied; couldn't afford to look bad on TV.

The bailiff bid them rise and come to order for the Honorable David M. Ray, Superior Court Judge. Right on cue, he entered with confident manner, reflecting his style of arbitration. Both prosecutors and defense respected his impeccable fairness and scholarly interpretations. So they rose in honor, out of genuine respect, not merely protocol. He sat down.

"Good morning. For the record, both sides are present, and the jury is seated, along with our two alternates. Good morning to the jurors."
He read the headliner.

"We're here today for the State of California Versus David Isaiah Eastbrook. Mr. Eastbrook, you are charged with the following violations of the California Penal Code"

Judge Ray cleared his throat, preparing to read the charges, straight from the CPC.

"Section 207 (B), kidnapping of a child, 187 (a) murder with malice aforethought, 261 (a) & (2) rape, while it is accomplished against a person's will by means of force, violence, duress, menace or fear of immediate and unlawful bodily injury on the person or another, 288.7 (a) sexual intercourse or sodomy with a child who is ten years of age or younger, section 289. (a) (1) sexual penetration with a foreign object, when the act is accomplished against the victim's will by means of force, violence, menace or fear of immediate and unlawful bodily injury on the person or another, (I), when the victim is under16 years of age."

He took a sip of water; too many years of reading the same verbiage eroded vocal cords, as well as spirit... the main occupational hazard for good judges.

"Additionally you are charged with possessing huge quantities of obscene matter, section 311 (a); "obscene matter, means matter, taken as a whole, that to the average person, applying contemporary statewide standards, appeals to the prurient interest, that, taken as a whole, depicts or describes sexual conduct in a patently offensive way, and that, taken as a whole, lack serious literary, artistic, political or scientific value."

When he finished, there was a recess. The courtroom buzzed. The jurors were going to try a real pedophile, murdering sonofabitch. Cathy O scurried out to report. The wonderfully fog-diffused sunshine would highlight her eyes.

Court came back to order fifteen minutes later.

Val De La Vega stood. She didn't use notes... she didn't want them distanced; she wanted the jurors sniffing maggots, ready to kill the bastard from the get-go. That was her reason for personally trying this case; and with her upcoming gubernatorial bid, a few hundred hours of primetime coverage wouldn't hurt, either. She straightened her already straight jacket, careful to expose her cameo to the camera, stopping right on the rehearsed X taped on the floor.

"Ladies and gentlemen, my name is Valeria De La Vega. I am the District Attorney for White Sand County."
Then she pointed at the defendant.
"And that man, David Isaiah Eastbrook, is on trial for the unspeakable charges Judge Ray just read into the record. First of all, thank you for taking the time to hear this case. I know it's a burden to sit such a lengthy trial, and I thank you."

She faced the jury.
"The evidence will show that the defendant kidnapped Tiffany Michelle Simpson. The evidence will show he had her in his RV. It will show he raped her with a foreign object. The evidence will show that the defendant killed her and dumped her body high in the mountains of Mendonesia County, California."

De La Vega went back to her table, letting her words sink in. The courtroom was shocked into silence.
"The evidence will also show that the defendant was in possession of many pornographic images of children... Now, this is a court of law; you must find on the facts and His Honor's instructions. I believe that when you do, you will agree... David Isaiah Eastbrook is GUILTY on all counts. Thank You."

De La chose a short opener, even though the court was prepared for one that might take hours... but it would be a long trial, with plenty of time to drive her points home later. Besides, she had seen trials where the prosecution failed to live up to a few small promises. Before the defense finished, the small-hills looked like Mount Everest. Reasonable doubt was easily cultivated in such fertile soil. So she decided not to give Freely a chance to pick at empty promises. Besides, her crew signaled; time for a commercial.

Judge Ray despised long opening statements. While remaining unbiased, he couldn't help but stick a tiny gold star next to Val's name. She was not only comely, but competent and concise. It was a pleasure to have such a lawyer in court. Too bad they weren't all that good.

He turned to the defense table.
"Mr. Freely, are you ready to proceed?"

"Yes, your honor, but may I suggest a short recess?"
"Good idea; we'll resume in fifteen minutes."

The court emptied fast. Some folks hurried for a smoke. Jurors sprinted to feed parking meters, six blocks downhill. Everybody went to empty coffee-strained bladders. Then, virtually everybody gulped more coffee before court came back to order.

But of them all, only Paul Freely remained stationary. The moment the bailiffs left the courtroom, he slid open his cell phone.

"Racer X?"

"Yeah..."
"I need you, good squire!"

Dan Sciacca grabbed two copies of the disc and hopped on his scooter. He was about to make legal history. Speeding through the busy streets on his moped, the hacker made excellent use of sidewalks and spaces between gridlocked lanes. Freely met him outside the rear of the courthouse, the only place free of marauding media.

"Hey... *did you bring it?*"

He nodded eagerly as he drained his third Red Cow of the morning; he was pumped. Just as the empty swished into a recycle can, he yelled.
"Yah... got two copies, like you said... and I hacked the dates, just like you..."
"*Shhhh!!!* Careful, son... *careful!* The bricks have ears, boy! What you *MEANT to say* was... the date that *appears* in the properties section shows WHEN WE FIRST LEARNED OF THE VIDEO, which was *YESTERDAY,* RIGHT?"
"Oh, yeah... right!"

He replayed the lesson, wherein counsel coached the shit out of him; never give 'em more than they ask for. Make 'em prove it. Never assume they know what we know. Never chat or blab... *to anybody.* Sure, Racer X knew what he wanted him to say.

The client's security-cam footage had a superimposed date; they didn't mess with that, but the date in the properties section was another matter; he changed it, to make is seem like Defense just found it last night, instead of four days earlier.

If the People had enough time, Freely feared they'd find the hacked date, so he wanted to spring it on them at the last minute. He counseled Dan on the next move.

"Ok, sit in the hall and wait for my call, and DON'T talk to *anyone.*"

"OK"

Charles Pees Freely walked briskly into court. He too, was about to make legal history. The court came to order. Determined to upstage De La Vega, he walked to the X and mugged for Anchorpussy's camera.

"Good morning. my name is C. Paul Freely. I represent the defendant, Dave Eastbrook. I compliment the People for a succinct, logical opener; in fact, I agree with most of it!"

The room buzzed; unaccustomed to hearing defense counselors agree with the State. He raised a finger skyward. The buzz quieted, eager to hear his conditionals.

"She thanked you for your sacrifice; I too, THANK YOU. She asked you to listen to the evidence, and again I agree. Counsel also advised you to rule on the facts, and I agree on that, as well."

He straightened his tie; time to get serious.
"The District Attorny asked you to find Mr. Eastbrook guilty, and again... I AGREE... *PROVIDING* that the facts in evidence *prove him guilty!*"

The place buzzed even louder. Freely let it sink in while De La squirmed; she had no clue where he was going, but Val hated surprises.

"BUT FAIR'S FAIR... IF *NO FACTS PROVE HE'S GUILTY,* then you must find my client *NOT GUILTY.* I'm sure his honor will instruct you about this, as well."

He gave the cameras a full-face, trying not to smirk, thinking about his secret weapon.

"Counsel also said this is a court of law, NOT REVENGE OR HATRED OR BIAS; YOU MUST RULE *ONLY THE FACTS AND THE LAW.* Thank you."

He sat down and keyed his text message to Racer X in the hallway; time to bring it!

The prosecution shuffled papers; they weren't prepared to start so soon, because Freely usually gave long openers. Judge Ray prompted them.
"Does the prosecution wish to proceed?"

Meanwhile, Dan entered and handed a bailiff the disc. The bailiff carried it to defense counsel. De La Vega stood up to address the Court.
"Your Honor, the People call Darwin Townsend."
"Objection, your honor… *sidebar?"*
"Come forward!"

Before the camera swung to the defense table, both lawyers scurried to the bench. Judge Ray spoke first.

"You're objecting to this witness being called, Chuck?"
"No, your honor, I'm objecting to the entire case the state has wrongfully brought against my client."

Now it was De La Vega's turn to look surprised.
"WHAT? On WHAT grounds?"

Judge Ray chimed in; "Yes, on what grounds?"
De La Vega noticed the inflection; "OH, sorry, judge."
He smiled; "It's OK; heat of the moment, and all that."

Freely produced the CD.
"On the grounds that I've just come into evidence of prosecutorial misconduct, wrongful interrogation, illegal search and seizure, judge. Give me time to crack the books and I'll have others too, Judge."

All the while, De La Vega vigorously shook her head.
"*Bullshit;* sorry... Perhaps *chambers, your Honor?*"
He was way ahead of her.
"Indeed, chambers... *now.*"
He turned the mike back on.
"We'll take a twenty-minute break."

The courtroom had been deathly silent, as if to hear their whispers, but only the parabolic mike caught the conversation; and, since it was illegal to eavesdrop, it was officially turned 'off.' Cathy O mentally squirmed, trying to think of a way to out the scoop, but it was too early in the trial to piss off the judge.

Everybody that needed a smoke, coffee or piss break hauled ass. Cathy O spoke rapidly, delivering news to her unseen audience.

"A most unusual side-bar occurred, BEFORE the first witness took the stand... We are unsure what it means, but as the news breaks, you'll hear it first here... This is Cathy O, LIVE... from White Sand County Superior Court, Room One!"

SIDEBAR

Inside chambers, Judge Ray sat down heavily and poured coffee; he loved his home-ground Mexican blend. He lit a cigarette, but this time it had little taste. Nasty surprises always did that.

"Ok, sit down... Chuck, what have you got?"

Freely didn't really know the best way to show his royal flush, so he just slow-rolled one disc onto the oak desktop and the other to De La Vega.

"Your honor, this video proves the search was illegal."
De La Vega seethed at being sandbagged.
"*BULLSHIT!* Your honor, he must've…"
Judge Ray waved her off.
"Plenty time for that later... Chuck, would you play it?"

He booted the judge's video system. The screen powered up, showing a nighttime view of a single person approaching, under a streetlight.

Freely hit Pause and prefaced it.
"Your honor, this face gets clearer later, belongs to Sarah Blacklock; Gander City PD forensics unit."

He hit the button; the image continued walking out of view, under the RV's roof-mounted cameras. Then a new angle showed her skulking inside the darkened Winnemako, obviously taking samples.

"Your honor, notice the built-in date caption; this search occurred five *weeks BEFORE* the People had a warrant; it speaks for itself, Judge."

All eyes fell on De La Vega.
Her thoughts raced; how the fuck did Freely get that copy? No, she couldn't say that; her people already destroyed their copies. No, she couldn't say that, either. She needed time. She was fucked.
Images of her gubernatorial campaign faded out, replaced with handcuffs and prison bars. She panicked.
"*How the FUCK* did you get that?"
But before the words died, she hated herself.
"You mean *BECAUSE your guys destroyed yours?*"

Now Judge Ray was keenly interested.
"Yes, Chuck, *how DID* you get that tape?"
Suddenly Freely was on the defensive. He decided to keep attacking; it worked before.

"Your Honor, as the People are aware, Mr. Eastbrook stored his images in a hard drive, at his residence. The people *HAD TO BE AWARE* of this, because their... for lack of a better term, *"legitimate"* search warrant later included his electronic stuff."

He paused, waiting for an objection, but De La was too busy thinking how to stop the hemorrhaging.

"What the People didn't know was that my client *ALSO* uploaded his surveillance videos, et cetera, *to a dedicated remote storage location.* If your honor orders me to disclose the location I will, but I'd prefer to keep it confidential, as it could aid my client's defense... *SHOULD* we need to mount one."

Judge Ray shrugged.
"Keep your secret for now. We've got bigger fish to fry."

Freely felt bolder now.

"Poisoned fruit, Judge; I'll be filing motions to suppress... the search, confession and of course, to dismiss with prejudice and possibly a motion to sanction Prosecution for this egregious act of misconduct. But for now, suffice it to say, I object to the entire case brought against my client, Your Honor."

Val felt the first wave of nausea... Medaris and his rogues; she'd worried that the scam could go south. Now it *wasn't just south*, it was the fuckin' Antarctic.

She did notice that Freely hinted he might stop short of prosecutorial misconduct. Of course, his honor could open that can of worms by himself, but all she could do was try to be sincere; an innocent oversight from a huge office staff...

She tried not to puke while struggling to buttress her imploding fortitude. This would be her worst hour, but worst hours never lasted; that's why they called them 'hours'. She vowed to come out of it somehow.

Judge Ray summed it up.
"Well, this is a fine mess we've stepped into. We haven't heard a witness and we're already in a big vat of shit. You guys want a drink?"

He pulled out some Sour Mash, poured some in his coffee cup and two shot glasses.
"Go ahead; we won't be out of here any time soon."

Both lawyers grabbed the drinks. Judge Ray sipped before speaking.

"Well, I see problems, some larger than others. But before you write those motions, Chuck, let me save the taxpayers a trainload of money. First, let's fry the small fish, Eastbrook's civil rights.

I'm ready to set that perverted sonofabitch loose, and God knows that really frosts my balls to free such a scumbag… and we're off the record here, *SCUMBAG SONOFABITCH."*

Both parties were stunned by his candor.
"It'll cost my bench. Nobody wants a judge that lets a serial child killer go free! The voters won't forget; my opponents will make damned sure of it!"

He took a bigger sip.
"And it's sure as hell going to cost Val a shot at the governor's mansion. That's a damned shame, Val, California could use you."

He drained his coffee, refilling with pure hooch.
"Then Chuck, you'll be the perverts' hero of the hour. Then, I'll be forced to order an inquiry about your video, with regards to authenticity and *WHEN* you discovered it; if you sandbagged Val with it, just to ham it up for TV… well, do the math."

Freely's guts churned; Juge Ray smelled a rat.
"I'm ready to set him free, but The People have a huge public safety issue here; Serial killers ought not be walking the streets, stalking fresh victims. I'm giving the People fair chance to show if they might have discovered Eastbrook's sins *WITHOUT* the tainted evidence. If they can, Chuck's motions would be moot and the confession would be in again."

The judge frowned pensively; he was looking for outs.
"You both knew about that *first* bloodhound; scented his RV a month before?"

Both counselors nodded.

"So, if the People would've inevitably discovered that original point, *THEN* you'd have something."

De La Vega felt a huge burden lifted; the judge was tossing her the keys to her career. If the man wanted a blowjob, she was ready.

Freely's voice quashed her gratitude.
"Please *Your HONOR, you KNOW this* is reversible! My client…"

"Oh, don't give me that 'my client' crap; save it for the cameras."

Judge finished his booze; the session was over.

"I'll tell you one thing… it looks like we all had better start covering *some serious ass.*"

RECESS

The best judge in Southern Cal addressed the court.

"Ladies and gentlemen; some UNUSUAL points of law have come up, which speak to the very core of our legal process. I'm giving both parties time to research these important points. Court is adjourned until Monday, Nine AM."

He instructed the jury; keep quiet about the case, no talking about it to spouses and media. Spectators buzzed, heading into the school of preying sharks, microphones and cameras trolling the baitfish. Most of the teams envied Cathy O, standing inside the emptying courtroom, speaking so excitedly into her camera that she missed the woman by the windows.

"Well, this most unusual proceeding has everyone in a quandary! The Defense team, headed by C. Paul Freely, objected to the State's first witness being called. I've covered many trials, but it's a new twist for me. More, at eleven; back to you, Vince."

She flashed her best dimple-smile as the scene faded.

TAILSPIN

Val's brain slipped into a tailspin, not entirely from the whiskey; her career was on final approach to a burning terminal. Stall buzzers sounding loudly, she decided to just add some flaps and power and wing it straight for the smoking carnage. She hadn't made it this far by dodging danger; that always caused more damage later.

The first flaming loading gate was the throng of reporters, cameras and microphones running toward her; she decided to head it off. She grabbed the nearest electronic dick and pulled it to her glossy lips.

"We have just been made aware of new evidence. To ensure a fair trial, Judge Ray called a recess so both sides can review it... The People have no further comment. Thank you."

De La Vega's quick exit left the surging crews with more questions; it wasn't like her to miss a chance for airtime. They quickly adjusted, sprinting for the exiting gallery, defense counsel or anyone who might give them a sound byte worth airing.

She headed for home, but when she pulled up to the curb, two news vans rolled around the corner. She gunned the 'Vette straight for the mall. The side doors opened into the fast food pavilion. Twenty-six metal tables planted in concrete. She picked the cleanest table and rested her forehead in her slender palms.

The food scents hit her. She ordered an espresso and bagel, thinking it might absorb the alcohol. Halfway through the snack, her thoughts began to clear. She felt calmer upon discovering her brains hadn't completely left her… yet. Plans started forming. First, get the CD to her people; if it was altered, she might be off the hook. Well, not all the way; there was still the matter of misconduct.

Val tossed her trash in a can and took a much-needed stroll through the mall. The fashions had changed since her last stroll… what was it, six years? Eight, since she'd bought anything other than suits. Her window reflection proved she was out of style.

But she couldn't stop the images of her next set of clothes; orange jumpsuits with an off-white name patch, set off with satin-black leg irons and chrome plated handcuffs.

She groped for options; she could jump in the shit and take it like a man... tell the judge the naked truth. It would be painful and brutal, but at least it would be swift. The the sentencing phase, based upon prior complaints, gravity of the act, her degree of involvement in it. Oh, yeah, and of course, the amount of damage to the accused.

So far, the damage to Eastbrook was limited; sure, he was wrongfully accused, vilified, searched and jailed, but it wasn't like he'd been executed. Aside from the inevitable civil suit, there was little to fear from Team Eastbrook. If she called off the dogs, they'd stop barking. Besides, he'd be too busy defending other charges to come after Val; *maybe.*

Option Two was the lawyers' stock and trade; deny, deny, *deny!* Anybody in her office could've lost it. An underling might have inadvertently tossed the disc… Who could say?

Blaming others was a seductive trap, but any judge worth the salary could spot lies a mile away. Besides, reporters lived for such fiascoes. The longer a story held their interest, the deeper the investigation went. Such a story could skyrocket a reporter's career.

She vowed to never let a cub reporter piss on her grave. Far better to spill her guts in one monumental instant than let them pick her bones for a month straight.

Then again, if she were to come clean and THEN infer some type of interoffice mismatch, it might be enough to win the judge's heart. She quickly formed the test-dodge.

'Yes, your honor, I'm to blame, but gee whiz, judge, it's a big office with lots of cases. I don't know who lost the tape, but damnit… what's one tape, versus the value of putting away a baby-raping serial killer? Besides, we would've obtained the evidence some other way… Not sure how, but… Oh, and I'm sorry and I won't ever do it again… now let me curtsy and smile… Blink, blink.'

It wasn't much, but it was all she could come up with. She shopped for other options; couldn't find any…

It was a bad day at the mall.

SEXTORTION

Freely and Eastbrook sat in conference, the radio twanging country music, as usual.
"What happens now, Chuck?"
"We dropped the bomb; it's their turn to sift rubble."

Seeing his metaphor miss, Freely expounded.
"Well, the DA's shittin' her pants; she's got problems. Not as big as yours, but prosecutorial misconduct is big, especially when the charge is so compelling."
He stood and paced while he sorted it out.

"She'll drop your case, to minimize fallout. Val wants to be governor; the sooner she puts this in her rear-view mirror, the better. IF they can prove my man hacked our discovery date, we're as dead as last week's meat loaf. But Racer X says their dudes aren't as good as he is. Remember; the state already had it, then they *conveniently lost it.* They'll be too busy covering their ass to worry about cooking yours."

"Judge Ray has problems, too. If he dismisses, he'll never get re-elected. If he tries you, he'll get reversed... and NO JUDGE wants a capital trial reversed. It's fair to say none of us have ever seen a trial scenario like this one."
The lawyer moved closer to his client.
"Speaking of which, we need to think ahead; you have press coverage across the nation... Let's assume you'll be a free man soon... you'll need to start calling lawyers in every city you've lived, so remember."
Eastbrook smiled weakly.
"I'll remember."

"Good. I'll see you later."

Freely drove home. His door was ajar. He caught a whiff of Cathy O and spied her black silk panties draped on the mantle, candles on the counter. Silk teddy-covered nipples peeked around the bedroom doorjamb. Anchorpussy was ready to fuck another clue out of him.

Undressing as he walked, he could only marvel at her cunning in breaking into his place; his locks were the finest money could buy. But then, so were those breasts. It was a fun game, tits versus wits.

He tried to remember to be cautious. Then her remaining lingerie dropped to the hardwood...

The game was over; tits 2, wits zero.

SCRAMBLE

The weekend passed too swiftly for De La Vega and her hackers. Apparently, the video was just as authentic as those they already destroyed.

But they did manage to discover the whereabouts of Eastbrook's secret e-storage. Actually, they should've found it the first time, if only they hadn't been so busy trying to put their illegally obtained forensics into play.

Fallout Nevada, population sixty, was Eastbrook's sham storefront; just a small cinderblock shed, adjoining the post office. Inside the building with rattle-can frosted windows were the barest cyber-necessities, tirelessly storing filthy skeletons by the gigabyte.

Six thousand gigs of kiddy porn clogged the DA's computers when the filthy cyber-closet disgorged its disgusting contents. Time wouldn't permit viewing one-tenth of the images. There were shots of anal penetration, cunnilingus, vaginal sex, every position and scenario imaginable, torture shots and defecation shots ad nauseum. She scarcely contained her hatred, because Val already knew that first thing Monday morning, Judge Ray would have to set the mother of all child-killers free.

To make matters worse, the grapevine outed her affair with Medaris. Knowing his honor's strict code against sleeping with peace officers, it was just gasoline on the fire; the conflagration would burn her career to ashes.

The more she struggled, the clearer it became. She would lose her job. She'd never become governor. She might serve time for conspiring to wrongfully convict. Her private phone was jammed with calls from the press; vultures, eager to peck her smoldering corpse.

But one thing kept her from sucking a gun barrel; there was a sliver of a chance that things might go her way... delusional thinking, certainly, but Judge Ray hated pedophiles too. Perhaps he could find some wiggle room.

All she could do was try to get some sleep and face the threat head-on... She never backed down before. There sure as hell wasn't any point in starting now.

CHAMBERS

The DA awoke to the message machine beep, a full three hours before court time.

"Val? Judge Ray; you're probably not sleeping either. I need you in chambers, 7:00 sharp. Thank you."

She got up and showered. It was odd, a judge calling in the wee small hours; maybe he wanted to get a jump on the media. Or maybe he found an alternative to the firestorm ready to consume them all.

Across town, another answer machine beeped. But this time, two sets of ears heard it, just before their second late-night orgasm.

"Chuck? Judge Ray; I need you in chambers... 7:00 sharp. Thank you."
Cathy O slowed her writhing hips for a second.
"SEVEN? Oh, honey... will we be finished by then?"

The look in her eyes said she was close to coming again, and would he dare leave her in such a horrid state? Something strange was going down, for the judge to call at that hour.

Freely groaned. He resolved not to come before Cathy did, which apparently wouldn't take long. Meanwhile, she resumed pumping for details with every hip stroke; he grunted 'em out, one word per thrust.

"Probly... got... deal... oh.... *GOD... YEAH!"*

Cathy moaned with synchronous delight; it mightn't be much of a scoop, but it *WAS* fun getting it this way. Fifteen minutes later, Cathy O primped for her camera while Charles Pees Freely headed for chambers.

Judge Ray's clerk had coffee ready. His honor arrived a few minutes later. He didn't have the robe on yet... just Levi's, cowboy boots and a Black silk shirt. He looked ruggedly good. His Honor didn't waste time on formalities.

"Thanks for coming in so early. I appreciate it. Listen, before you unload those motions I need to know more. First of all, *WHO KNOWS,* besides us?"

The question hung suspended, like a beer fart in church. De La Vega answered.

"A few cops; Medaris, Sangreal, Blacklock..."
"Yeah, I know about them, but *who else* knows?"

"My staff and Ledbetter & Smith; my cyber-sleuths, but they're loyal... They won't talk."

It was time for Freely to come clean.
"My hacker's a wild card; wants to be famous, so the world will know what a genius he is. But he's got ADD. In a few days he'll be hacking new gigs. I'll bet a sham deposition, a few pages of fake testimony with his name on it would do the trick. That, and a lifetime supply of Red Cow. The man's crazy for..."

"No, Chuck, the OTHER risk; your, uh, *current lover.*"

There it was, the mother of all lead balloons; the judge knew of his affair. But then, *who didn't?* Every man in SOCAL wanted to bone Anchorpussy, who *just happened* to be getting all the scoops.

"Well, I admit I leaked her a few tidbits, but nothing of any trial importance... just enough to keep her on the hook, so to speak. But not a WORD about the video."

De La Vega scoffed at the sex hound's despicable comment. But before she had time to regret it, the judge quietly raised a hand.
"We don't have time to get into who's screwin' who, but if we *DID,* I'd call Medaris in here."

"I'm sorry, your honor. You're right."
"You're damned right. But the key is for *US not to get screwed.* So again I ask; *who else have we got?"*

Both sides were silent; maybe the list was complete.

"Let's assume this is the whole roster. Cathy O is our biggest problem, agreed? Now, in a couple of hours, I have to let the defendant walk; the press will go into a feeding frenzy."

He spoke with surprisingly candid hostility.
"I'll cite the laws that compel me to let this conscienceless bastard loose. The press is going to gut me like a five-foot Yellowtail. Counselors, I'm not overstating it when I say... *I AM OPEN TO IDEAS."*

The trio thought hard, but there weren't any outs. They could only apply the law and let the chips fall where they may. Judge Ray capped the mood.

"You know, I value our free press, but I hate it when they go to such... wanton abandon to sell tabloids. But there's one thing about the press; it's predictably fickle... As soon as some celeb does something newsworthy, our 'front-page' story will line fifty thousand parrot cages. I've seen it happen before."

"If we can survive to the parrot-shit point, we'll be OK. Now, let's assume Cathy O knows some things you might have uttered in the throes of passion. This is clearly a breach of ethics, but the bigger point is... what can we do about her; or will it even matter?"

De La Vega opted to take a shot.
"Well, her career's on the line, too. She's got a network deal in the hopper; how would *THAT* turn out if they learned she'd been humping counsel for scoops? Chuck, I know you're not into blackmail, but..."

De La left it unspoken; they had the goods on Cathy O, once they started thinking like a woman. She got up and poured coffee for all three, starting with the judge.

"Now, correct me if I'm wrong, but I think it's in our best interests to just process this and get it over with. The more we dodge, the worse it will get. We all *know* where it's going. Why don't we just *get there?*"

In the end, they decided to do just that; get the tar baby off the bench, before they got stuck any deeper.

TURNABOUT

The bailiff seated the jury. He pushed a button; Judge Ray entered and sat down.

"I note that both parties are present, jury and alternates are seated. I am sorry for the delay, but it was unavoidable… you will soon see why."

He took a sip of water, but it didn't help much.

"Certain documents have only recently been discovered, which the Court was not aware of. These documents compel me to make a ruling. These documents prove that the defendant's Fourth Amendment rights were violated. For those of you who may be unfamiliar with the Fourth Amendment, I shall give a quick synopsis."

"The Fourth Amendment gives every person the right to be secure from UNREASONABLE search and seizure of their person, papers and effects… It is my considered opinion that the defendant's rights were significantly violated, which adversely impacts his Constitutional right to a fair trial."

He sipped more water, but it tasted dry.

"Consequently I am compelled to dismiss a great deal of the evidence against the defendant.. The People are entitled to continue, but must do so WITHOUT the illegally obtained confession and all evidence obtained from the resulting illegal search. Do the People wish to proceed?"

De La Vega stood, shaking with a mixture of rage against Eastbrook, and fear of what would soon happen to her career. She stuck her neck through the legal guillotine and squinted her eyes shut, knowing her words would trip the suicidal blade.

"Your honor, THE PEOPLE rest."
"Your Honor, the Defense rests."

The court buzzed. It took six blows of the gavel; "Order... ORDER!!!! It is my duty to..."

He faced the camera to drive home the salient points.

"But I am compelled to make a statement...Please come to order..."

The room slowly quieted, until he could be heard.

"In our system of law, the defendant has the unimpeachable RIGHT TO BE PRESUMED INNOCENT UNTIL PROVEN guilty. This cornerstone of our system, handed down from the constitution's framers, is the core of our society. An overwhelming sense of liberty dominated our earliest charters, establishing, preserving and securing a system of law which compels the state to make its case beyond a reasonable doubt or the defendant goes free."

"Sometimes the law seems like it doesn't work, but I assure you; it is the finest legal system in the world. It might set a guilty person free... And by that, I do not mean to infer that this defendant is guilty... But in an AMERICAN COURT OF LAW it is better to set a hundred guilty free rather than to convict one who is innocent. That is the spirit of our law, and this court absolutely... adheres to that spirit."

HE took a final sip, before dropping his bomb.

"Since the People have failed to prove their case, it is the order of this court that the case is dismissed, with prejudice; Mr. Eastbrook, you are free to go."

Eastbrook stood up, in celebration. The courtroom went ballistic. His honor banged the gavel over and over before it got quiet enough to hear him; "I remind you all; this is a *COURT OF LAW!*"

Five sequential explosions shattered the air; the courtroom was shocked into silence. The petite woman stood in the gallery, her smoking Ladysheriff still pointed at the dying pedophile. She corrected the judge...

"NOW IT'S A COURT OF JUSTICE!"

She dropped her gun, raised her hands; within seconds, the diminutive divorcee was in custody.

Buffy Rutherford noted with glee that nobody moved to help the rapist/killer motherfucker. She enjoyed watching him bleed out, sprawled over the defense table, a few frothy pulmonary bubbles rising from the bloody holes in the back of his suit.

Cathy O's camera, already aimed for Eastbrook's reaction, got the bullets slamming into his perverted backside. The commotion knocked over the camera after that, but by god, she had her first syndication scoop.

ALLOCUTION

"When I saw that smirk on TV I knew he was the one that stole my baby girl. And I knew he'd go free. Decent people always pay when pedophiles play."

With steely resolve, Buffy stifled her grief, determined to give a factual account. If Brittanie were to be remembered, let it be for something good... and killing Eastbrook had definitely been a good thing. Hers would be a memorial of truth and justice.

"We go... *we used to go* to pageants... She had a real shot at Cottonwood; made the final cut. I remember him getting out of his car so we'd all get to the elevator at the same time..."

Her eyes darkened; she hesitated. Her lawyer gently prompted.
"Go on, Buffy, please."

"He led us to a private room. We thought he liked her for the finals; but he liked her for his next victim."

Her voice cracked; they let her grieve until she regained control.

"While her peers were qualifying at Saint Albion's, we were at the morgue identifying her body. My life was never the same. Lance left me; neither of us could deal with the pain. Nothing will ever ease my aching heart or bring Brittanie back..."

Her eyes filled with fire.

"But I can't tell you how *wonderful* it felt to watch my bullets rip into his repulsive body... How *GREAT*; like waves of extreme, hot orgasms."
Her lawyer tried to intercede, but no dice; Buffy wouldn't hear of it.

"We had an ugly divorce, but I was too fucked up to worry about who got what or how much the lawyers gutted us for... I just grieved and tried to find a way to ease my pain."

Her lawyer relaxed; her client was paving the road to an insanity defense, in case the allocution deal somehow went bad. With each sentence, Buffy paved another lane; a fuckin' crazy-bitch superhighway.

"My boss and customers got sick of hearing about my problems. I got fired, but I didn't care; I felt I was being punished for being such a lousy mother."

"When I think back, we really were to blame. We got absorbed in the pageant bullshit... we would've killed to get her into the finals. Come to think of it, we did."

She shook her head.
"Now I see it... We dress them up and sex them up. We display them for pedophiles... Lord, forgive me... "
The ADA tried to refocus Buffy.
"Oh, don't be so hard on yourself; you had no way to know he was a pedophile. He fooled everybody!"

But she heard it a thousand times before in her head.

"Wrong! A mother's *JOB* is to protect her children, not pimp them. Spare me the platitudes, counselor; I tried them all... and they're *all full of shit*. I failed her the way a mother should never... And if I go to jail, I choose to think it's for abusing my daughter, not for killing that scumsucking child raper!"

Then her eyes got steely.

"But you're interested in how I did it, right? I bought a Ladysheriff, in 38/357. I wanted to load 357's, but my shooting coach said they had too much risk of pass-throughs; I didn't want anyone else to be harmed, so I loaded 38's."

I practiced 'til I could keep all five in the chest. The practice sessions helped ease my grief, so I practiced a LOT. My groups finally averaged four inches at 25 yards; better than most of your officers."

Laura Stark raised her eyebrows; under lethal combat stress, it was definitely some disciplined shooting.

"You want to know how I got my gun past the metal detector and inside court, right?"

Stark nodded silently.

"Yeah, I'll bet... that was my biggest obstacle."

Buffy sipped water, ready to spill her guts.

"I rented a pickup in Yuma, then I drove to Gander City. I went to jury selection; with so many strange faces coming and going, I blended. I sat in the rear by those big windows, with the cranks? It took several recesses before I finally managed to crack one open without anyone seeing me. It didn't set off any alarms, so I knew I had a chance."

"I stayed away until the jurors were seated, then I double-checked; the window was still cracked open, so I knew nobody paid attention to the windows."

"I bought one of those extension pruning tools to prune high branches; you know the ones?"

Stark nodded, too absorbed in the tale to interrupt.

"I bought tape, rope and plastic pipe, with bell ends, they slip together... Then at last call cops were busy chasing drunk drivers. I hid in the bushes and taped the pruners to the top pipe. I tied rope to it.

Then I inserted the revolver and tested it; the release worked great. I assembled the pipes and thought I was good to go, but I didn't know pipe bends like spaghetti... So I raised one length, then slipped the next into it, and so on."

"I had to lean it against the building. I walked it away from the wall to angle the thing toward the windows, until I finally heard it touch glass. I triggered the shears and heard my gun hit rooftop gravel.

"The next day, when I peeked I saw my revolver, placed as perfect as if I laid it by hand! It was so close that I could barely see it under the windowsill. Nobody else could either, unless they knew where to look."

She smiled a cold, bloodless smirk.
"After that, it was easy, *except for waiting*; the urge to shoot him was almost overpowering, but the prosecutor hated him too. I decided to give her a chance. I've heard that pedophiles don't have it so easy in prison. It sounded like better revenge than a few quick bullets."

"But after hearing her opening statement, I lost all faith. She fell short, describing the bastard's actions against my Brittan... I mean the Simpson girl... *fuck it... against them all!*"

Paula Martin interrupted her client.
"Say, can we take a break? I've got to pee!"

When the room emptied she implored her client.
"Buffy, if you're not going to tell them about the handkerchief, the allocution's no good... for god's sake, *STOP RIGHT NOW!*"
"Don't worry; I can't stop. I'm not sorry, either."
She motioned for the officer to take her to the john.
When they resumed, Buffy Rutherford hit full stride.

"I smelled a rat when I heard the defense opener. What's his name, Freely? He seemed too confident. I knew the fix was in. Hell, *anybody could see it!*"

Paula was glad not to have a Buffy Rutherford on any jury; she was too good at reading people.

"Then they went into chambers before the first witness was called; they were cooking up a deal, and the bastard was gonna get off. I was so glad I had my gun; I don't know what I would have done, without it!"

The ADA squirmed at the thought of an armed citizen.

"Then the judge said some bullshit about new evidence... It sounded like; *'we're studying loopholes, to see if we can let him go.'* I was so pissed off, I wanted to shoot 'em all. It was a long fucking weekend."

"And then, Monday comes; sure as hell, the judge lets him go. I waited for some people to get clear. I emptied the gun into him. That's it, isn't it... *ALMOST?"*

She had one last ace to turn, her only bargaining chip. Her lawyer noticed the hesitation.

"Might WE have a moment?"
The People left the room. Paula paced, pumping her client.

"Buffy, tell them *EVERYTHING* about the handkerchief OR you'll stand trial."

She knew it... *She wasn't stupid,* but it seemed so disloyal to betray her anonymous accomplice. Besides, her conscience tried to convince her that jail might ease her pain. That's what her lawyer was fighting against. Conscience; what a bitch.

"Buffy, Honey, prison time won't make it go away; you agreed to tell *everything,* remember?"
She nodded, but her heart wasn't in it.
"You HAVE TO tell them about that fucking rag… *or we're screwed!"*

The hanky was a big security concern. It reeked of collusion; or maybe conspiracy to commit murder. Anyhow, it reeked.

"OK."
She had to trust her lawyer's judgment. They called for the People, who by the way, brought her a cold can of Coke; they hated Eastbrook, too.

"OK, I'm going to tell you everything *I know* about that handkerchief, as part of the deal we made."

Both sides nodded, careful to have their nods caught on the lens behind the one-way glass.

"Before I reached for my gun I checked the bailiffs; Smith, Perkins and Creekmore's eyes held hatred, probably born of impotence to do what they really wanted, which was to kill that sonofabitch. Then, Barrett's eyes… They held happiness."

"Then while everyone was watching the judge, I reached for my gun but the window was locked! I looked back and saw a handkerchief on the windowsill. I felt my gun under it. I grabbed it, rag and all. I checked to see if it was still loaded… I guess that was dumb, because *WHY* would someone unload it but *leave it there?* I can't tell you how relieved I was to see my bullets smiling up at me from the front of the cylinder, happy to go to work on that cock-sucking daughter-murderer. I forced myself to focus on the job, so I wouldn't hurt anyone else."

"I heard the judge talking about Eastbrook's civil rights and it being a COURT OF LAW. When the motherfucker stood up, I waited for some people to clear... It seemed like a long time... like a YEAR!"

She took a sip of Coke, smiling coldly.

"I put the first three in his lungs, avoiding his spine; I didn't want him paralyzed, falling before I could shoot the last two into his ass."

"I wanted him to feel his balls blown off. The first three were frangible loads, preventing pass-through. The last two were core-bonded hollow points, to penetrate, then expand. I hope they blew his fucking cock and balls off. Maybe you could fax me the coroner's report?"

Her audience was too absorbed to answer her ghoulish request. She drained the rest of the Coke.

"Anyhow, THAT'S all I know about the handkerchief. I don't know WHO put it there. Could have been ANYBODY. Who has access to department-issue handkerchiefs? Officers, their wives, janitors, laundry workers?"

"Given the number of angry parents in Eastbrook's despicable past, could it have been a parent? "

She was on a roll, buoyed by possibilities.
Did I act in concert with any other person? No."
She drained the coke and tossed it in the trash.

"You asked earlier if I KNEW the bailiffs; Hell no! I tried to avoid 'em, so I could shoot the filthy scum-of-the-earth that murdered Brittanie and left her in a dry storm drain to rot, like so much... garbage."

"I barely know which name-tag goes with which badge. Like I said, Barrett's eyes looked happy, but I heard he had a vacation planned, before this trial crashed his plans. Maybe he was happy to resume his vacation. You might wish to think twice before you ruin his fine young career with a witch-hunt. If there's one thing this whole thing taught me about, it's loopholes."

With that, Allison 'Buffy' Rutherford complied with her allocution-for-immunity deal. The Prosecution had been trumped again.

But, if the truth were told, they had little interest in finding her anonymous co-conspirator, aside from the security issue of how the hell she managed to smuggle her gun past metal detectors, two plainclothes guards and four alert bailiffs.

Except for that, they were just going through the motions, so when Anchorpussy stuck that black dick microphone in their faces, they'd have something to say that was actually true, for a change.

AFTERMATH

David Isaiah Eastbrook lived thirty-something seconds after the first bullet struck; long enough to hear someone say; *"Now it's a court of JUSTICE!"*

And although her last two hollow points missed his genitals, she was pleased to later read the faxed M.E. report; the fourth bullet ass-raped the serial child killer, exploding his Sigmoid colon, Common Iliac artery and Prostate. Just before he bled out, Eastbrook's final thoughts summed up pedophiles' recidivism problems;

"At last... I'm cured."

Jennifer Simpson moved in with her honky-tonk boss. It might have worked, too, but three months into their relationship, a drunk driver tee-boned her Ford. Ironically, she died from a liver laceration.

De La Vega lost her law license, but once free of the Bar's restrictions, spoke her mind freely. The voters didn't care if she was screwing Medaris or if she lost her license. Californa had way too many lawyers, but not enough leaders.

As for her part in the cover-up, it made her more popular; Val bent a few rules to grill the serial killer, and they loved her all the more for it. Her bumper stickers, paid for by a coalition of parents of abducted kids really turned the corner.

"MAKE VAL YOUR PAL."

Charles Pees Freely sold his practice and Testarosa. He moved to Barbados, bought a Moped and maintains an international pay-per-query legal advice website. He still counsels perverts... I mean *"alleged"* perverts, and they still pay four times the going rate. With his profits, he bought a beachfront bar; He finally has enough Mimosas to wash down the taste.

Three weeks after arriving in sin city, Steffanie Walker died of an ephedra-related heart attack while auditioning horizontally for a really big show. Her last orgasm wasn't exactly 'choke-sex', but it was quite intense just the same.

John Medaris retired, plays poker with his redneck buddies, fishes for steelhead and hunts Black-tailed Deer in the mixed forests of Mendonesia County. He stays in good shape, awaiting a call from the governor.

Tim Dockins continued to interrogate suspects; he sublimates the stress by shooting on the Sheriff's traveling pistol team, and gives weekend seminars for women in defensive shooting skills.

Racer X lives peacefully in a Zinfandel vineyard in northern California, free to hack away in peace and prosperity; besides, the landlord said cats are OK.

Shit flows downhill; Dunn, Sangreal and Blacklock were fired for their part in the evidence scandal. Eric and Sarah broke up, shortly after he fell asleep and she found the ass scratches and the hickey on his pubes.

Eric and Kaylee married, raised dogs and lived happily ever after... but compared to the time they were horny naked strangers pressed against the cold kennel wire in the moonlight, the sex was never again so good. But then, is it ever?

Buffy Rutherford became a firearms instructor for the National Association of Gun Owners in Sangre De Jesus, New Mexico. She trains women in self-defense. Her gun of choice; the Ladysheriff. She splits her time between seminars and lecture circuit, alerting pageant parents to the risks of pimping their daughters for camouflaged pedophiles.

The pageant circuit went on as usual. Once assured the lion was gone, the herd went back to blissful grazing. Judging would be up to Agustus J. Hightower... and everybody could trust *HIM*. After all, he'd been a preacher, earlier in his career, *hadn't he?*

Well, I hope that you liked my book; if you didn't, tough shit... At least I got your money.

Seriously, I welcome ideas 'n good reviews.

Hell, I might even send you one of my *other books* for your effort.

Now put the book down.

Go take a shower and have a drink; you earned it.

- ➤ COURT OF LAW; a crafty serial pedophile hunts, hides and preys. To catch him, three young cops must think outside the profile. Filled with sub-plots, quirks, sex, depravity and corruption; pretty good twist ending, too.

- ➤ CHAMELEON; a young serial killer with father issues; his dad's a famous profiler. Just as chameleons use camouflage, Vincent stays invisible by exploiting profiling data. A few twists, weird sex & bizarre ending.

- ➤ TURNABOUT; a hunter stumbles upon a cartel Pot patch, high up in the coastal mountains. A gunfight ensues, which sets Ted Morgan on a grisly course of payback. Warning to cartels; it's not wise to piss off your average American hunter... Turnabout's such a bitch.

- ➤ Urik-Tah, the Death Rose; Majesty travels at Hawk Speed to see what happened to a mining colony. She finds something that will change the balance of power in the universe. If you like Star Trek, you'll like this. Has the mother of all unexpected endings.

- ➤ Mother saves Majesty; Read the Death Rose first, then this prequel. It might warp your mind. Key ingredients; theoretical speeds, black holes, primitive life-form weaponry, insoluble conundrum.

* Owing to various online production glitches, books are either in print now or will be online shortly, at the biggest book site; can't say the name, but it's... *amaz*...ingly big. Search author or title; hell, you'll figure it out.

BTW; I'm always receptive to ideas from readers, for stories. I welcome ideas, love praise... and scoff at criticism.

Lanceksteele@yahoo.com